DUCCIO AND THE MAESTÀ

By Gail Tanzer

Front cover: The Siena Cathedral
Photo by Gail Tanzer

Back cover: scenes from the Palazzo Pubblico and the streets of Siena
Photos by Kris Perkins

Front and back cover designed by:
Jill McClain
Design 23

THIS BOOK IS
DEDICATED TO MY FOUR LITTLE MUSES
(you know who you are).
Thank you for inspiring me with your
spontaneity, creativity and zest for life.

PART ONE

JUNE 9-12, 1311

CHAPTER 1

JUNE 9, 1311

Shortly before the crack of dawn, Duccio di Buoninsegna finally fell asleep. Just at that moment, the artist heard a heavy Clump, Clump, Clump on his workshop door. Duccio bounded out of bed and down the stairs to greet his expected guest: Arnolfino Buccini.

In a scratchy voice, Duccio said *"Buon giorno,"* and Arnolfino responded in kind.

Duccio walked over to the reason for their meeting and looked down at it, saying, "It looks damaged lying on the floor in pieces like that."

Putting his arm on Duccio's shoulder, Arnolfino said, "I know, *Signor* Duccio, but we will put it back together again in no time---just as we planned. We could never have gotten all of it in one piece out of the door."

"I know, I know," said Duccio with a faint smile, "I must go upstairs now and prepare for the day."

As he walked back up the stairs and entered the room he shared with his wife, Duccio shed his nightshirt and donned his new tunic, belt, stockings and cap. Although the materials of his outfit were not of the high quality he would have preferred, they were what Duccio could afford. His wife, Taviana, rolled over in the bed they shared, brushed away a ticklish piece of straw that had escaped from under its muslin covering and said with a smile, *Buon giorno, mio sposo*, are you ready for your big day?"

"I hope so," Duccio replied as he looked down at his wife. "You know how the Maestà has consumed me. I just hope the people will like it."

"Do not fear, my dear. They will love it just as I do when I look upon it."

"I hope you're right, Taviana, I hope you're right." Then Duccio smiled at her, pointed to his clothing from head to toe, bowed a little and said, "Now, how do I look?"

"Quite handsome, my dear," Taviana said in a less-than-enthusiastic voice. Although Taviana regularly complimented her husband on his art, she never expressed admiration for his appearance. She knew that his finely chiseled features, blazing blue eyes, graying but full head of hair, and muscular frame could make him an apple prime for the picking in the eyes of other women. Taviana knew of women as well as men who, despite all of the priests' warnings of damnation, let their minds and emotions stray to others besides their spouses. But Duccio usually cared little or nothing about how he looked. He was so involved in his art that he let his hair and beard grow out in uneven lengths, and he wore clothes that were paint-stained from top to bottom. Taviana knew that women seldom gave him a second look.

However, in the last couple of days, Duccio had spent time at the mirror slashing and then delicately cutting his hair until it actually looked neat. Although Taviana realized his efforts were all in preparation for this day when he wanted everyone to love his Maestà and have some respect for him as its artist, she didn't trust the motivations of women who allowed themselves to stray.

"Quite handsome, is that all you can say? I think I look *marvellous* for a change, but that's not the important thing. What matters is that the people like my Maestà," said Duccio. "I must go now. I will see you after the installation." And as he was walking towards the stairs, Duccio turned back and called, "Wish me luck."

Taviana harrumphed, "Luck? I would rather just say God bless you today, but since you believe so much in luck, I will say, *Buona Fortuna,* my dear."

At that moment, the high-pitched call of one rooster aroused the other roosters in the area, and all of Siena rolled out of bed as one. Floorboards squeaked, babies cried, metal pots jangled, and everyone seemed to be preparing for mass and then work. But there would only be mass today. Instead of work there would be a parade, a government ordered day off from work, and the installation of the Commune's long-awaited Maestà.

Duccio went back down to his workshop where his former apprentices---Ambrogio and Simone---had just entered and were talking about their tasks ahead. Then Duccio's assistant Mimmo and Arnolfino's son Tommaso arrived. The mooing of the neighbor's ox could be heard as its owner and driver waited for their precious cargo.

Arnolfino, Duccio's master carpenter, moved into the center of the workshop and said loudly to everyone "*Allora!* For the last couple of weeks we have gone through the motions of how we would transport the Maestà. As you know, it will be a very delicate procedure. There is no room for error. May Almighty God bless us in our endeavor."

All of the men crossed themselves and said, "Amen."

"And so now," Arnolfino continued, "Let us get into position to take the first half of the Maestà very carefully outside and place it on the oxcart."

On cue, the men picked up the first half where each had previously been instructed to grasp it and then slowly carried the eight by sixteen foot piece at an angle out the workshop door. It fit---but only barely--- through the opening. They brought it to the oxcart where the neighbor was ready to drive his faithful ox through the Commune to the final destination of the Maestà. The men lifted this section and pushed it up against the inner edge of the oxcart. Sweat dripped off of the assistants as well as Duccio and Arnolfino, and they breathed a collective sigh of relief.

Then they reentered the workshop to get the other half of the Maestà. As they were guiding this part through the doorway, Mimmo tilted it too much, and one of the pinnacles brushed the corner of the door with a slight screech.

Duccio yelled, "Mimmo, Mimmo, be careful!"

"I am so sorry, *Signor* Duccio!"

Duccio examined the slightly nicked area and saw that it would never be noticed. Then he said, "All right, just watch it."

After the men transported the piece outside, they lifted it up on the oxcart.

Arnolfino reminded them, "Slowly squeeze this half against the other half and keep applying pressure there throughout the journey."

Although this was a long oxcart---ten feet in all---only two feet of the second half of the Maestà rested on its wood floor. Just as Arnolfino said, the men would have to keep pushing and squeezing the second half onto the first half until they got to the church where four more men were assigned to meet them and help them carry the Maestà up its steps.

Just as the men finished positioning their precious cargo, the morning mass bells rang and people across the Commune streamed out of their dwellings and onto the streets, but they were not going to mass immediately. Instead they assembled on the parade route to view their long-awaited Maestà. A few citizens stayed back and decided to scrutinize the Maestà from their upstairs window openings. Everyone wanted to get in the best place possible to get a good look at the altarpiece.

According to instructions from the governmental leaders, the bell ringers from each of the forty Sienese *contrade* (neighborhoods) pealed their bells at the same time. Everyone hung out their *contrada* flags and their finest tapestries. Trumpeters, drummers, and minstrels stood ready to entertain.

Duccio smiled when he saw the normally drab streets filled with so many spectators

Along the Parade Route

and entertainers. They all came to life when they saw him with the oxcart ready to begin the procession.

"Well, here goes," Duccio said to Arnolfino. "They will either love or hate my Maestà, and I will have to be ready for whatever happens."

For the second time that morning, Arnolfino reassured him, "Do not worry, *Signor* Duccio. Everything will work out fine."

The Council of Nine governing body in Siena had asked Duccio, as the artist, to march behind the oxcart and wave to the people as the Maestà passed by. *Never before has an artist received such recognition in our Commune*, Duccio thought. *We are usually considered as little more than bakers or cobblers even though we have a gift from above…but, thankfully, things have been changing since we entered the Trecento* (thirteen hundreds).

In the throngs of people lining the streets, Duccio did not see Arnolfino's daughter Elisabetta and his wife Anna who had scurried from their *contrada* across the Commune so that they could be near the beginning of the parade route. Elisabetta initially positioned her mother and herself on the side where they could see the front of the Maestà. Elisabetta knew all about the altarpiece and thought that her mother---who adored the Blessed Virgin---would like to see this side of the altarpiece first, for it depicted Mary sitting in Majesty on a throne holding her child Jesus and surrounded by a myriad of saints and angels.

Before the Maestà rolled by them, Anna said to her daughter, "I am a little afraid…it is so crowded."

"What could happen, *Mamma*? We are all one big happy family today in love with the Holy Mother and Baby Jesus."

Her mother grabbed Elisabetta's hand and then pointed to the Maestà as it made its way to where they were standing. "It is gigantic, Betta! Oh, and look at how beautiful it is. The Blessed Virgin looks so…so… holy, and she and the Christ Child are almost as big as you and me."

An onlooker next to them wept and waved a handkerchief to the Virgin while saying, "Bless us, dear Mother of God."

A child of about four pointed to the child Jesus and grinned.

Everyone was clapping in response to what they saw as the oxcart passed them by. This led to ripples of cheers down the *via* as others anticipated the arrival of the altarpiece. Walking behind the oxcart, Duccio breathed a deep sigh of relief.

Anna pointed to the four once-martyred patron saints of Siena each kneeling before the Virgin. "Remember our four patron saints who I have been trying to teach you about? Look at how *Signor* Duccio has painted each one with…"

"I know, I know, *Mamma*. I'll never forget your nightly bedtime story about how Ansanus was beheaded for baptizing people in Siena," groaned Betta.

"Oh, and look, Betta, in the second row around the Virgin, there are other great ones: St. Catherine, John the Baptist…"

The oxcart started rolling too far for them to take in the rest of the Maestà. As they were losing sight of it, Anna sighed.

Elisabetta said, "Let's walk with the cart so we can look at it some more."

Anna protested, "But people will get angry if we walk in front of them."

"Don't worry, *Mamma*, we'll do it quickly."

And so, with a little elbowing and a few apologies, they continued to study all of the details on the front of the Maestà.

"That section along the bottom of the Maestà is *interessante*. I see that it shows a lot of scenes of Jesus' childhood," said Anna.

"That section is called a predella, *Mamma.*"

"Sometimes it helps to have an artist in the family," her mother said.

"Ssh, *Mamma*, someone will hear," Elisabetta said, as she looked around her. "Do you see on the top the scenes of Mary when she was a child?"

"Glory be to our Holy Mother," Anna said as she crossed herself. "All of the colors on this whole side of the altarpiece are so bright. And it looks so… so… rich with all of the gold in the painting."

"Oh, yes, that gold," said Elisabetta under her breath as she remembered her experience with the gold.

"Look, and there's a row of men looking like the disciples…" her mother said.

"No, they are apostles," responded Elisabetta.

"Whatever you say, my child," said Anna with a little grunt. "Don't you like those pointy sections too with the faces of angels and the one really big pointy part with Mary's beautiful face?

"Pinnacles, *Mamma*, those pointy things are pinnacles." She hesitated before she looked at her mother and asked her, "And what do you think of the angels?"

"*Dio mio,* Elisabetta, those angels are so dear with their sweet eyes. They look like they really adore the Holy Family."

Elisabetta chuckled to herself as she treasured her little secret about the angels. She was glad that her mother liked them but was also relieved that she did not venture a guess at the identity of who modeled for them.

Then Elisabetta pulled her mother forward past the cheering crowds to run in front of the oxcart and take her to the other side of the street. This would enable them to view the reverse side of the Maestà together.

Breathing hard, Anna said, "You didn't tell me that *Signor* Duccio painted all of these pictures on the back of the Maestà." She hesitated and started counting. "There must be at least twenty of them. I know it took Duccio about three years to make the Maestà, but I would think that some painters would need that amount of time to just paint one of these pictures."

Elisabetta whispered, "There are forty three pictures, *Mamma*, and they all show scenes of what happened to Jesus in the days right before and after He was put to death."

"They are…what can I say?...*Incredibile*," said Anna with tears in her eyes.

Elisabetta took in the comments of the crowd. She heard people pointing at individuals in the scenes---like Peter or Mary Magdalene---and saying, "That looks like someone I have seen."

Christ Entering Jerusalem

Well, it probably is the face of someone you have seen, said Elisabetta to herself, because she knew that Duccio sent his apprentices into the Commune to sketch common people for subjects depicted in each scene.

Then one of the spectators viewed the painting of Christ Entering Jerusalem and shouted, "Look, that looks just like one of our city gates in Siena!"

Anna also commented on the same scene: *"Dio mio,* Duccio painted our black and white insignia on the wall right next to the gate! And look at those towers, Betta, they certainly look…well, they certainly do look like the ones right here in Siena. Oh, how I love this side of the Maestà also, Betta…" As Anna pointed to all the people who were clasping their hands together and cheering, she exclaimed, "Isn't it nice to see everyone together and so happy today?"

In fact, the citizens of Siena were so absorbed in studying the Maestà that they only gave the artist a passing, but grateful, wave. A few noticed Duccio's blue eyes---they were usually the first part of his appearance that strangers noticed. One woman, who momentarily locked eyes with his, thought to herself, *His eyes look like they are looking right into my soul.*

Despite the challenges presented by the hills and irregular cobblestones of the Sienese streets, Duccio's men did a perfect job of balancing the Maestà on the oxcart. At the midway point of the journey, the men led the cart down a *via* with a sharp decline and paraded it around the Piazza del Campo plaza and in front of the Palazzo Pubblico government building so that the thousands waiting in the center of the city could behold the Maestà. Then the entourage brought the Maestà up an incline and through four city streets until it finally reached its destination---the Siena Cathedral---

The Ten Steps

glistening in its white marble walls with delicate pink marble outlining its portals and greenish-black strips of marble enveloping its sides.

When they finally halted the oxen, the carpenter and apprentices along with several other prearranged helpers began the process of taking the Maestà off of the oxcart and bringing it into the church. The men had to carry it up ten wide steps to the cathedral doors. Duccio went to assist them. As he was passing the oxcart, he unwittingly put his hand on the cart and pricked his finger on a stray splinter of wood.

"*Ahi!*" Duccio exclaimed. That hurt. But Duccio was doubly alarmed by this injury because he, like many others, viewed hurting one's finger as an omen that evil would follow. He felt he had suffered enough tribulations from bad fortune in the past. However, Duccio tried to dismiss this possible sign of bad luck and told himself, *This is turning out to be my perfect day. I am not going to let anything disturb me.*

Then, as Duccio and his men made their way with the Maestà through the wide church aisle, the artist felt more awed than ever by the cathedral's black and white pillars topped with gold adornments and paintings on the ceiling. For the first time, Duccio saw in person how his gigantic altarpiece with its bold colors and lavish gold would fit in magnificently.

Interior of the Cathedral

Standing near Duccio, Arnolfino held his breath until he and his men soundly lodged the 16 by 15 foot wood panel onto its pedestal. A hearty "*Bravo*" escaped from Arnolfino's lips, and he looked around embarrassedly because he knew he was in such a solemn place.

After the Maestà was put into its final resting place, Duccio stepped down from the platform of the high altar and blended in with the other male citizens all of whom were given small lighted candles and were told to gather around the front and back of the Maestà. Once the men became positioned, the women and children were allowed to approach. Thousands of worshippers were standing shoulder to shoulder.

Duccio thought to himself, *Hmm, I like the way the Maestà appears to glow with the flickering candlelight bouncing off of my soft blues, strong reds, greens and gold. Something that I had not planned but is working wonderfully. Bellissimo!*

From where Duccio was standing, he could see how clearly defined the gold letters were that he had written on the base of Mary's throne: "Holy Mother of God be the advocate of Siena's peace; be the advocate of Duccio's life who painted you thus."

The monks and priests standing at the altar gazed at the Maestà with smiling eyes even though they kept their serious demeanor. But then Duccio's eyes met those of one of the priests---Father Giacobi---who had just looked at the inscription and began scowling.

Father Giacobi thought, *Never before has an artist put his name on any piece of art---let alone on an altarpiece---which should just be to the glory of God and the Blessed Virgin.*

Duccio saw the aversion in the priest's eyes. The artist realized that some might think he was pompous in putting his name on Mary's throne, but he did it because he needed all of the blessings or luck he could get. *Perhaps Mary will respond favorably to my painted prayer*, he had said to himself. None of the other priests frowned when they set their eyes on his inscription. Duccio knew that Father Giacobi, who was on the planning committee for the altarpiece, had not approved of how he had designed the Maestà from its onset.

Peccato, Duccio thought. *This inscription could be trouble now.*

Duccio looked for his family in the crowd and ultimately laid eyes on a second person who did not look like he wished him well. This man almost hissed at Duccio when he caught his eye. A shudder passed through the artist's body. The hisser was Corporal Alessandro Olivetti, a man with whom Duccio did not share a love for the military. The corporal was responsible for much of what Duccio regarded as his previous disgrace and ill fortune.

And if Olivetti knew about Elisabetta, Duccio thought, *he would try to make my life a living hell.*

At that moment, the bishop slowly rose from his gilded throne and hobbled to the elaborate pulpit carved out of marble by Siena's foremost sculptor, Nicola Pisano. Priests fluttered around and tried to assist him, but the bishop motioned them away. As the bishop began his slow ten-step journey up to the podium of the pulpit, the cathedral was dead silent. Everyone seemed to be saying prayers in their hearts that their leader would arrive safely at his destination.

Once he made it to the top and regained his breath, the usually dour bishop donned a faint smile. Considering to himself that this might be the last piece of religious art that he could install, the bishop said to himself, *Almighty God has saved the best for last.*

The Pulpit by Pisano

"*Sia Lodato Gesu Christo*," the bishop chanted as usual.

"*Sempre sia lodato*," the people responded.

"This may be the last time I am able to address you," the bishop began, "and so I am going to talk with you as brothers...and even sisters. My days on earth are limited. You can see that for yourself. My knees are weak and my voice is failing, but today I feel as alive as a twenty year old, because looking for the first time at Duccio's Maestà, I feel pure joy. Oh, this altarpiece is certainly the largest altarpiece in the world as we all expected, but it is also the most beautiful that I have ever seen!

Most of you have attended mass every morning until the work bells peal. You love the Lord, but when I have visited early mass and seen your downcast heads I know it is not so much in regret for any sins you have committed as it is from your being half-asleep.

But now, thanks to the artist Duccio di Buoninsegna, you will look at an altarpiece that will lift your heads and provide a feast for your eyes. One could study forever the detail that Duccio has put into each hand, face, and piece of clothing. And, most importantly, you can reflect on our Blessed Mother, our Savior, and each patron saint and apostle who has served the Lord---many to the point of dying for Him.

When you gaze upon the back of the Maestà, you will be reminded of what Jesus went through from the time he entered Jerusalem until He hung on the cross to die, and then arose from the dead. Oh, what He suffered to save us from our sins!

And if the spiritual aspect of the Maestà doesn't completely command your attention, the richness of the gold in the background and in the robes should dazzle your eyes…just as they do my cloudy ones.

But, perhaps most importantly of all, you will feel comforted as I do gazing upon those sweet angels who embody God's love for us… as well as…as well as for the Blessed Mother and Baby Jesus. The front of the Maestà gives me a glimpse of what it will be like when those angels take me to my heavenly home…in the not too distant future.

As you know, we commissioned Duccio di Buoninsegna to create the Maestà to commemorate our victory over the Florentines fifty years ago. On that day, every woman, child and old person came to our cathedral and prayed to a wooden statue of Mary to give us victory. Many of you remember that day as I do"…The priest's eyes lit up, and he stretched out his arms as he swayed a little. "And she did, our Blessed Mother gave us the victory even though we only had 25,000 men and Florence had 35,000 men. A day we will never forget!"

Tears rolled down the bishop's face, and he faltered for a while until he concluded his address, "Whenever you look upon your beloved Maestà, pray that the Virgin in her infinite mercy will preserve Siena in the future from any and all enemies, traitors or misfortunes."

Then the bishop raised his arms as far as he could and chanted, *"Dominus Vobiscum."*

And the people replied in a loud, heartfelt voice, *"Et cum Spiritu tuo."*

Then all of a sudden thousands of hands of the grateful believers struck together and made the church sound like it was exploding. Babies yelped and old people shuttered, but it was all music to Duccio's ears. Both tears and laughter shook him at once.

Duccio felt something like pure joy coursing through his body. He thought, *Over the years, I have felt like a failure in many ways. I've felt like I brought disgrace upon my dearly departed father's name----Buoninsegna. Some of my actions have been anything but good. Yet, if my mother and father still were alive they would both say that today I did well.*

Duccio snuck out of the cathedral before the service was over. All he wanted to do was sleep. He took a side door out of which he knew he could exit. As the artist escaped, he had to pass by the cathedral's front again to get to the *via* towards home. He looked back and up at the gigantic, circular stained glass window he had designed for the upper story of the cathedral some twenty years earlier.

Since the service was still continuing inside, there was not a soul outside except for one beggar balancing himself with a crutch against a short pillar on the bottom of the church steps. As the artist gazed at his window, he took note of the beggar and saw one of his legs was missing.

In like manner, the pauper took note of the escaped worshipper. The beggar, who ate or starved according to the kindness of strangers, fancied himself an expert at weighing a man's soul in a moment's notice. Within a glance at the potential giver, the beggar saw a man of average height, slender but strong, slightly stooped with longish black hair having silver streaks. Over his lavender tights, the man wore a dark blue tunic with a thin row of embroidery at its neck and sleeves, and he carried a purple hat with a feather in it. Even though his clothing was somewhat festive for the occasion, it did not smack of wealth. What struck the beggar most were the man's eyes. This aging man had blue eyes that looked unusually youthful and wide open. They seemed to be seeing things that were in the man's inner world as well as the external here and now. The beggar felt that he couldn't quite predict whether he would obtain alms from this one: he seemed kind enough; he didn't look poor; but he seemed to be in another world.

Then the man pleased the beggar by walking a few feet towards him and looking as if he would give him a couple of *denari*. Instead he asked, "Did you view the parade with the altarpiece? I did not have much of an opportunity to see the Maestà, because I was pealing the bells of the church in the San Ramon *contrada*," Duccio lied. "By the time I got over here to see it, I had to stand way in the back of the cathedral and could hardly get a look at it."

"Oh, *Signore*, it was nothing like I have ever seen. You can see that my life is pretty hopeless, but when I looked at the Holy Mother and the angels, I felt God's love."

"*Bene*," replied Duccio. "Did you find anything else of interest about the altarpiece?"

"With the shape I'm in, it's hard to get around, but I did see that it had a painted back too."

"Oh, yes, and what did it look like?"

"There were many, many…what would I call them? I guess you could say they were picture stories of our Blessed Savior doing things with people…"

"And what did you think about them?"

"*Interessante*, they were very *interessante*. One of the people in the stories even looks like a beggar who is a friend of mine."

"Oh, the characters looked that real, did they?" asked Duccio.

"*Si, Signore*…And now it looks like…perhaps… you are about to give me alms."

"*Certamente*," said the artist, as he took two *denari* from the little moneybag under his tunic.

When the beggar received his alms, he asked, "And, *Signore*, when I am praying and asking the Holy Mother to bless you for your charity, who may I say was so kind?"

The artist began walking away, then turned around and called, "Duccio di Buoninsegna!"

Knowing that this was the name of the artist who had painted the Maestà, the beggar almost fell from his perch,

Then Duccio proceeded home with a spring in his step while he prayed, *Dear Lord (if you are really up there), please forgive me for needing the approval of this humble beggar in addition to all of the adoring worshippers on the parade route…I am sorry I am so vain, but I am greedy for a reward after these three long, hard years.*

CHAPTER 2

JUNE 10, 1311

After a night of celebration with his family, Duccio felt fuzzy but functional sitting at his workshop desk the next morning. Mimmo was sweeping up shavings of wood, nails and other debris left behind from the Maestà. Elisabetta was at the markets trying to sell a little quantity of left-over gold.

A noisy stir awakened Duccio from his reverie. He heard his neighbor Ignazio imploring Mimmo to let him inside.

Mimmo hurriedly brought Ignazio to Duccio's office door and said, "Someone is here to see you, Master Duccio."

"*Mio amico* Duccio," began Ignazio as Mimmo slowly returned to his sweeping. "My life may be in jeopardy!"

Duccio got up, closed the door and inquired, "What do you mean, Ignazio?"

"Two messengers from the Council of Nine delivered to me a summons this morning and it said, from what I could tell, that I must appear in court tomorrow to face the charge of tr...tr...treachery."

"Ignazio, that is quite serious. I know that sometimes at the *taverna* we talk about politics and that you---like me----," Duccio's voice quivered a little, "don't always side with the Ghibellines in Siena, but I doubt that anyone would accuse you of treachery for that."

"I must admit that there may be some truth to their charge," said Ignazio. "My weaving business has been going poorly. I went to Florence a few months ago to try to sell some of my tapestries. A man at the markets bought one and said there would be more money for me if I could work with him on something."

"Oh, and what was that something?" Duccio frowned.

"A spy party from Florence wanted to find a way into our city, but the man said they needed someone at the *Porta Romana* gate to get the other gatekeepers to look away for awhile so that they could sneak in. Because my business is not going well, my wife and children often go hungry..." Ignazio let out a sob, " I asked one of the men who I thought shared my political views if he would distract the other keepers for awhile on a given day so that..."

"You didn't," Duccio said.

With his head bent low, Ignazio said that he did and that the man whom he thought was a friend reported him.

"What can I do now?" Ignazio asked as his body began shaking.

"You know what will happen to you if you are found guilty, Ignazio. You will be tied to the tale of a donkey and dragged through the piazza..."

"I could take that and endure," said Ignazio.

"But then you would be hung upside down from a tree limb until you expire."

"*Dio mio, Dio mio,*" Ignazio said as he fell to his knees.

"You must flee Siena," Duccio advised. "Either go by yourself or take your wife and children with you. You have a brother on the outskirts of the city, don't you?"

"Yes, I do, I do. I am going now, *Signor* Duccio. *Grazie*," Ignazio said as he stood up quickly and ran out the door.

Mimmo came to the door and said softly, "Ignazio seemed upset, Master Duccio."

"Yes," replied Duccio. "Seeing your family go hungry can make you do some desperate things. Forget you ever heard any of this, and go back to your sweeping, Mimmo. Sometimes the less we know about certain things the better."

Then Duccio felt a dark cloud looming over his head. *Have I said too much at the taverna? Sometimes I have argued that I can understand why those Guelphs in Florence want the Pope to rule our region even though our Sienese Ghibellines think that the Holy Roman Emperor should be our leader. But I would never go so far as to betray our Commune. Those Florentines make me angry anyhow, because what they really want is our wealth. They are jealous that we have the Via Fracigena running through Siena with all of the pilgrims and traders the road brings in. I had better keep my mouth closed at the taverna from now on, though, or someone could set a trap for me. And I do have those two enemies…"*

❦❧

When Duccio closed his workshop for the day and plodded up the stairs, Taviana remarked, "Your footfalls don't sound like those of a greatly loved artist tonight. You just had the day of your life yesterday. I would expect you to be bounding around like a ten year old boy."

"Well, I am happy…in fact, overjoyed…about how things went yesterday. But I did have a bit of bad news today," Duccio said as he sat down across from Taviana at their oak table in the cooking area.

Taviana put her chubby little hand around Duccio's and inquired as to what the news was. Duccio told her of Ignazio's big mistake and how that put a fear in him.

"But, *mio sposo*, you would never commit treason against our beloved Commune, and everyone knows how much you love Siena and want to see her guarded from enemies… through your magnificent Maestà."

"We were so joyous last night that I didn't want to disturb the mood by telling you how at the installation right in church Corporal Olivetti shot me a look that was…well…venomous," Duccio said with his head sinking down slightly.

"*Ach!* You know that Olivetti is a strange one. He can't do anything to you now that you are beyond the age of serving in the *contrada* militia."

"If only I had gone to all of his drills…"

"But you did go to many."

"Yes, most of the men felt like me that the corporal was calling us together so much that we couldn't get our regular jobs done. If I would have stayed in his *contrada* and gone to every last one of his drills, I would never have had the time to think and create my art…and that is…well, it's my life besides you and our children."

"Remember, you went to most of the drills, *mio sposo*, and you would have gladly served if we had to fight the Florentines."

"*Certamente,*" said Duccio as he lightly thumped his fist on the table and then stood up and paced around. "But you know how Olivetti wouldn't let it go…how he showed up every time I was brought up in front of the magistrates for an unpaid debt…"

Before Taviana could launch into her periodic scolding of Duccio for his tendency to indebtedness and the time he was fined for loitering with his drinking friends after curfew, Duccio continued, "Something else happened at the installation…Your favorite priest, Father Giacobi, gave me a very disapproving glance when he looked at what I had written on Mary's throne."

"I did warn you that perhaps you were going a little too far with that."

Duccio scrunched up his face and said, "Well, the other priests and even the bishop showed no disapproval of it yesterday."

Taviana stood up and put her arm softly on Duccio's back, "Have a nice supper now, my dearest, and get some rest after Angelina and the children go to bed. You're just tired, and you know how you worry… and…and… think too much."

Duccio smiled at her, and just then his daughter-in-law entered from the bedroom where she was saying evening prayers with the children. All of

Duccio's six remaining adult children were married and on their own, but his son Tommè died two years previously when he fell off the top of a roof while sweeping a chimney. His heartbroken wife came with her two little ones to stay with the equally grief-stricken Duccio and Taviana.

Duccio and Taviana always tried to be cheerful around Angelina and the children, but sometimes their less-than-happy feelings could not be hidden.

"*Buona sera.* You look distressed, dear father-in-law," Angelina said.

"Oh no, Angelina, I am just hungry and tired. I will eat a little supper and retire early."

CHAPTER 3

That night Duccio was able to shake off his worries and sleep soundly. In fact, for the next few days he felt like he was walking on air. People on the streets greeted him with a smiling "*buon giorno*" or "*molto grazie.*" Duccio took long lunch breaks, afternoon naps and leisurely strolls in the early evening, but nevertheless the feeling that Father Giacobi was angry with him was like a minor toothache that just wouldn't go away.

A week after the installation on a night when sleep eluded him, Duccio replayed his history with Father Giacobi. He envisioned as clearly as possible every interaction he had with the priest when they were both on the Maestà planning committee.

Four years ago on a stormy spring day, Duccio had walked through its sculpted marble portico to enter the Palazzo Pubblico. A guard ushered him to the second floor of the building and opened an ornately carved door for Duccio to enter the room in which he would meet with the magistrates and two priests on the committee. Duccio took his seat at one of the

straight-backed, stately
wooden chairs that the magistrates used for all of their
meetings.

After everyone arrived,
the head of the committee
began, "*Buon giorno* to all of
you. We have been entrusted
to plan what is to be the largest altarpiece in the history of
all mankind. We have cho-
sen Duccio di Buoninsegna
to be the artist, because he
was the designer of the marvelous rose window of our
cathedral and has created a
well-received array of *cassoni*

Portico of the Palazzo Pubblico

(chests) and archive covers for our governmental records. Our task is to consider further how Duccio should paint our Commune's altarpiece."

Duccio had his ideas but bit his tongue until he heard the opinions of
others.

After a short period of silence, Father Giacobi began, "'Several years ago
I visited a city-state to the northeast---Ravenna---near the sea, and I observed
the majestic Byzantine art in their churches. Have any of the others of you
been to Ravenna?'

They all shook their heads "no" except for Duccio.

The priest continued, "I was awe-struck when I saw the great Emperor
Jus...Jus..."

"Justinian," Duccio said.

"*Si*, Justinian---from a few hundred years ago..."

"Seven hundred years ago, to be more exact," said Duccio

"I think I can explain this quite adequately on my own, *Signor* Duccio," said
Father Giacobi. "Anyhow, the emperor was shown in a mosaic at the San

Byzantine Art at San Vitale

Vitale Church. He was standing about eight feet tall holding a large golden bowl for the host to be used at mass. The bishop of Ravenna was holding a huge golden cross, and several church officials were holding symbols of our faith like a book with the Gospels. And then there were soldiers who bore a shield with what I think was a Greek cross..."

"So, Father, with all due respect, what is your point?" asked the chairman.

"Speaking as a priest, I believe that people need these forceful...you could say imperial... imperial images to make them respect the Lord and the Holy Mother and...and...to make certain that they behave properly...or else the wrath of God and the whole government will...come down on them."

The rest of the committee members frowned slightly and didn't say anything. They looked towards Duccio.

Duccio wiggled a little in his seat and said in what he hoped was a respectful voice, "Father, I greatly admired the artistry involved in making those Byzantine images---especially since most of them were made out of thousands of tiny pieces of mosaic tile." Duccio held his fingers together to show the size of them and smiled. "That art definitely has a place in history, but it was man's version of God over the last seven hundred years. Now, in our new day and age, I think we need change. I would like to portray a more loving... may I say...a more human God."

The priest cleared his throat, frowned and said, "And how exactly would you do that?"

"I would depict Mary and Jesus in a profoundly sacred, almost Byzantine manner, as you so wisely suggested, and I would make it look somewhat like other recent Maestà altarpieces that show Mary in Majesty."

The priest dropped his shoulders a little and said, "Good."

Duccio went on, "But, unlike other Maestàs, I want to show Mary and Jesus looking at each other with a fondness of sort."

"I guess I can live with that," said the priest without much enthusiasm.

Duccio sat on the edge of his chair as he went on to explain his vision for the rest of the altarpiece. "Angels, there would be angels gathered around the Mother and Child, and these angels...I want them to look very human. I envision them having the most compassionate eyes radiating...yes radiating... great concern for Mary and Baby Jesus, because they know what Jesus will face when he becomes a man. I want the worshippers to feel the warmth of God reflected through those angels."

As the other committee members nodded in agreement, Father Giacobi furrowed his brow but said, "I can live with those angels, I suppose, although I think it could lead to coddling Christians...and that could lead to weak moral behavior...if the people think God will take care of them...no matter what."

The rest of the committee members kept their silence, as they listened to the debate between the priest and the artist.

Then the other clergyman on the committee said, "*Signor* Duccio, as you know, the altar of the Siena Cathedral is not pushed all the way to the back of the church like in most other churches. When we have large crowds, people stand at the back and sides of the altarpiece as well as in front of it. Would you put anything on the back of the Maestà?"

"I did think about painting the back of the altarpiece for the reason you suggest, Father. I thought about depicting Jesus in the thirty days or so leading up to his crucifixion----Jesus eating and drinking with the common people, Jesus washing the disciples' feet, Jesus riding a donkey into a city that looks just like Siena..."

"Must you include activities that show our dear Lord in such mundane activities?" interrupted Father Giacobi in a shrill voice as he tightened his shoulders again. "I think you should depict Christ in his more powerful moments such as when he was feeding the five thousand, walking on water…or maybe…raising Lazarus from the dead. And why show him on streets like we have in Siena? Didn't his activities center around Jerusalem?"

Duccio responded in a quiet, even tone, "I want people to know that Jesus is not a faraway deity to be feared but…how can I put it in words?…I guess you could say a loving God-man who is right now with us in Siena."

Giacobi gritted his teeth and said, "My biggest fear is that you will use unsavory characters from the streets as models for the disciples like you did in your little Maestà sitting in the east hall of our Palazzo Pubblico right now!"

One of the government officials responded, "But I like that Maestà. The characters look so real, and you know our Council of Nine leaders encourage…what I would call…a sense of equality among all of us."

Giacobi was ready to interrupt, but the director of the committee spoke up loudly, "All right, we have heard enough debate between Father Giacobi and Duccio di Buoninsegna, although it has been thought-provoking. What we need is to come to a decision as to whether we want to use a strict Byzantine style or …or possibly a newer style combining the Byzantine with a softer message…"

Then Duccio interrupted loudly before the chairman reprimanded him: "That young, famous artist from Florence named Giotto is gaining acclaim for depicting Jesus' followers with real emotions in settings that people recognize. Just take a trip to Padua and look at his frescoes at the Arena Chapel."

The eyes and ears of the committee members perked up when they heard the names of Florence and Padua---two of their rival city-states---linked with this new artist Giotto doing such well-received art. The contract endorsing all of Duccio's ideas for the Maestà could have been signed at that very moment.

The chairman said, "I think that we can all agree that Siena needs to be at the forefront of art as we build more churches and government buildings. Master Duccio has already demonstrated his considerable talent. And, Father Giacobi, with all due respect, I have not heard anyone else criticize Duccio's small Maestà at the Palazzo…"

The priest tried to say something, but the chairman continued, "So, all in favor of going ahead with Duccio's concepts for our magnificent Maestà say "aye."

Everyone replied with a hearty "aye" except for one priest who knew he was outnumbered.

After replaying these events in his mind as he lay in bed next to his gently snoring Taviana, Duccio concluded that the priest was probably not angry just because he had put his personal prayer on Mary's throne. Most likely he was additionally dismayed, because Duccio had portrayed everything the way that he had predicted he would---and this portrayal went against the core of many of Father Giacobi's deepest convictions.

Am I being too suspicious, though, by imagining that this man of the cloth would take his displeasure to the point of doing something to punish me? But that's because another man of the cloth---the cloth being a uniform in his case---has sought repeatedly to punish me because he did not like what I did. Peace...Peace of Mind... ...that's all I want... that and maybe to stay out of debt and keep the Buoninsegna name in high regard. Then I wafted a question to the heavens, *Is that asking too much, Dear Lord?*

Hospital of Santa Maria della Scala

CHAPTER 4

Unfortunately, though, Duccio's fears were well-founded. On the very next day, after the first evening bell, Father Giacobi got ready to leave his domicile and do something about the Maestà. The priest resided with his fellow brothers at the Hospital of *Santa Maria della Scala* right across the *via* from the Siena Cathedral.

Brother Matteo, who was guarding the hospital door, said to the priest, "It's been a quiet day today, hasn't it, Father? Not too many ailing pilgrims passing through town this week."

"*Si*, Brother Matteo, I haven't had to give last rites at the hospital for a few days now."

Matteo responded, "And may I inquire, Father, as to where you are going on this lovely but sweltering evening?"

"I am going to take a long walk to stretch my legs, Brother Matteo. I will be home before the curfew bells peal."

Father Giacobi felt a little guilty about telling this lie, since he was really going to see someone who hopefully could help him make changes in the way people regarded the Maestà. *Ah, well*, Giacobi thought, *sometimes the end justifies the means.*

On this stifling evening, the priest felt itchy in his long, woolen monastic robe. He loved being a priest, but sometimes he envied men who on hot days could just slip on a light tunic and tights before going about their business. Secretly, he also envied men who could do one more thing---keep all their hair. As a child, Giacobi really wanted to be a priest, but he loved his curly black hair--hair that others said made his face look handsome. His one comfort, when he had to have his hair cut to be a monk, was that he could keep some of it, because he was in an order that mandated shaving of the middle of the head but left a fringe of hair around it. Although his fringe was starting to grow gray, it still had some curl to it.

I am so vain, the priest thought, and then he asked the Blessed Mother to pray to Jesus for his forgiveness. Father Giacobi walked down *Via Capitano* and turned left at *Via di Città*. He dreaded the rest of his long, hot walk up and down the stony streets to get to his destination beyond the Palazzo Pubblico.

Not being in the habit of going outside this late in the day, Father Giacobi had almost forgotten how dark the streets of Siena became when the sun was setting. With the city walls limiting the amount of land on which to build, residents had constructed second and third story wood additions to their homes--some of which jutted over the streets. These additions blocked much of the light from the sun. The dark brown and black hues of Siena in the evening were a far cry from the colors of the open fields that Giacobi knew as a child. The way the sun set over the grape vines in his vineyard created soft shades of green, purple and gold that he had not seen replicated even in the finest of paintings in Siena.

While the priest walked to his destination, he considered the man with whom he would soon be conspiring: Corporal Alessandro Olivetti. The priest had met the corporal for the first time in 1302 at the installation of Duccio's small Maestà at the Palazzo. Memories of that meeting flooded his consciousness.

The Palazzo Pubblico had just been built. It was gigantic and was right in the heart of the city. Its architects had designed it with a slight curve that meshed perfectly with the contour of the Piazza del Campo. This would be the impressive location where all public business would be carried out---taxes collected, babies registered, trials conducted, etc. Giacobi had been excited to see Duccio's piece of art, for it promised to emphasize how God, in the form of Jesus, along with the Holy Mother, was watching over everything that was being done in the city government.

Just the day before, Siena had heard about the installation from the heralds who announced its coming. Since Maestàs were a common piece of artwork in the region, people were not astounded by this news.

However, seeing as how he was a priest for the Siena Cathedral, Father Giacobi had relished the opportunity to view this small Maestà placed right in the house of government. After arriving at the Palazzo and finding the Maestà in the midst of a long hallway, he studied its front and back for some time. He literally bumped into a slender, frosty-haired onlooker wearing an immaculate *contrada* uniform with gleaming gold buttons.

Giacobi said, "So sorry, *Signore…*"

Olivetti straightened his slightly sagging back and said, "Corporal…I am a corporal! But that is all right, Father."

Giacobi then reverted to his usual squinting to see all of the details of the painting at a closer level.

Olivetti shook his head and muttered, "Mmm, mmm, mmm," but not in a way that meant what he saw was appealing to him.

"Are you having problems with this piece of work?" Giacobi queried.

Looking around and then putting his hand slightly over his mouth, Olivetti said, "Duccio should never again receive one commission from the Council of Nine to ever paint anything…never…never again!"

Looking at the man more closely, Father Giacobi thought he recognized the corporal from a hearing he had attended regarding fines that citizens---including Duccio on that day---had incurred. "Have I seen you before?"

"Probably, probably. I go to every hearing involving Duccio. Have you been to any of them, Father?"

"*Si*, I did happen to see him once at court when I went to plead for mercy for one of our regular worshippers who could not pay back a debt."

Olivetti raised his voice and said, "Duccio has not only been called into court many times for unpaid debts, but also he has disregarded the calls to muster in my *contrada* and others too."

Father Giacobi looked around to see if Olivetti was offending anyone, but Duccio was nowhere to be seen, and the few people looking at the Maestà did not seem to hear him. Giacobi whispered, "Good Corporal, I can imagine your concerns, but we had better speak quietly since this is kind of an austere place."

"*Si*, Father."

In a low tone, Giacobi said, "I am very concerned myself, although for different reasons. Looking at the characters in Duccio's painting, I see that he depicts the apostles and the women with faces of common citizens, some of whom I have seen in Siena."

Olivetti bent his head forward to study the painting's details and said, "Now that I look at it, I do see the faces of people I might know...there's someone who looks like Vincenzo the blacksmith and...oh, that looks like Rosa, who stands in that one doorway on *Via Capitano* calling to men... How dare Duccio! *Terribile!*"

"This shows a lack of respect, I think, for our Dear Lord and the Blessed Mother," Father Giacobi said as he shook his head.

"I think I remember you from a sermon or two that I heard at the Cathedral. I liked your approach. You are the one who really scolds us...I mean tries to remind us... about the punishments for sinning... even though you do it in a kind voice. Could that be correct, Father...Father...?"

"I am Father Giacobi, and yes, I believe that there are very clear rights and wrongs, but I do not want to be too harsh with the people."

Olivetti turned slightly as he heard the sounds of boots walking and people talking. "That's Duccio coming down the hall," he said. "I'm going."

He turned in Duccio's direction, grasped the handle of the sheathed sword that hung from his belt, straightened his curving back, and muttered a "Harrumph." Then he turned swiftly and marched away. Duccio recognized

Olivetti, shrugged his shoulders, and continued to walk with his companion towards the Maestà.

Having never formally met Duccio, the priest simply gave him a slight smile and took his leave.

Father Giacobi came out of his reminiscences about that day in 1302 just as he approached the tower in which Olivetti lived. He had not talked with the corporal since viewing the small Maestà, but he knew where Olivetti resided. A year or so after bumping into him at the Palazzo Pubblico he had given last rites to a woman next door to Olivetti and had seen him enter the tower.

Since he heard a noisy family on the first floor, Giacobi climbed the stairs in the vestibule to the second floor where he assumed Olivetti lived…probably alone. The priest lifted and dropped the heavy metal knocker. He heard someone from within plodding with heavy footfalls to the door.

The door opened slowly with considerable creaking until a man with hundreds of wrinkles peaked around it to see whom his visitor was. Olivetti said, "Good evening…who are you…a priest…? Oh, Father, I think it's Father Giacobi, isn't it?"

"*Buona sera. Sì*, I am Father Giacobi, but are you…are you… Corporal Olivetti?" Giacobi had to ask, because, if it was, the corporal looked decades older than he had nine years previously. Not only was his face as furrowed as a field but also his previously perfect-looking *contrada* uniform looked like it had been rolled through a field.

"*Sì*, Father, it is I."

"I was hoping that perhaps you could spare a little time. I would like to come in and share some concerns with you."

"Time, I have plenty of time…since a younger man took my place as corporal some years ago," Olivetti murmured as he ushered in the priest. "Have a seat." He motioned to a simple settee against one of the walls of the nearly bare living room. Olivetti crossed the room with a stiff-legged walk to his wooden chair placed next to a table on the other side of the room.

The former corporal cleared his throat and said, "I imagine that your visit has something to do with Duccio's new Maestà that they had the gall to put on the holy altar of our beloved cathedral. I know that you weren't any too admiring of the last one."

The priest nodded, and the corporal allowed a smile to cross his face. Giacobi thought, *Olivetti's smile looks sinister. What am I doing here?*

"I have been alarmed with Duccio's behavior since 1289..." Olivetti began.

The priest worried, *Perhaps Olivetti has been giving this too much thought if he remembers the exact year when his disdain for the aristt began.*

Leaning forward in his chair and holding onto his nearby cane with a white-knuckled grip, Olivetti continued, "In 1289, Duccio was fined five *soldi* for not being present at a meeting of the Council of the People. You know those meetings are required for all men of the militia to attend. Then two weeks later he would not swear allegiance to our *contrada* when I ordered him to. I had Duccio brought into court for this offense, and, thank God, he was fined ten *soldi*. He certainly did not learn...no, he did not learn from that first fine just two weeks before."

Olivetti huffed and puffed, "Everyone in Siena is loyal to his *contrada*, and all but a few show up for their military exercises."

He continued, "Once when Duccio was brought into court, the magistrate asked him why he didn't do his military service."

"And do you know what?" Olivetti raised his bushy eyebrows and pointed his cane in the Father's direction. "He gave the excuse that he was just too busy painting and setting up a workshop. Like no one else in the *contrada* has a job to do! The magistrate just smiled and let Duccio off easy, because he is Siena's beloved artist. Shame, shame on those magistrates!" Olivetti yelled as he thumped his cane on the floor. "Where was the justice? I ask you...where was the justice?"

The priest sat silently.

Olivetti stood up and paced back and forth as he said in a loud voice, "The magistrates would probably have overlooked Duccio's failure to repay his fines if it had not been for me speaking to them in private, over and over again, about how they should enforce the laws---even if it meant punishing their darling Duccio..."

Preparing himself for more exhortations about Duccio's infractions, Father Giacobi looked around the corporal's room. He saw some small wooden object lying on the middle of the floor. Also, despite the bare walls and little furniture, there was one luxury in Olivetti's abode: a slim window with real glass. *Why did Olivetti indulge in such a luxury?*

Although he noticed that the priest's attention was wandering, Olivetti continued, "My persistence paid off even though it took five years. On May 15, 1294, Duccio was called into court again and was ordered to pay a fine of eight *denari*, because---believe it or not---he still had not paid the fine from five years earlier for not attending the Council of the People meeting!"

"And then three short weeks later," Olivetti smiled as if he had just eaten a piece of the finest beef, "The magistrates gave him another fine of thirteen *soldi* and four *denari* for not paying off the fine from five years ago for refusing to swear allegiance to my orders. That was indeed a happy day for me," said Olivetti with a faraway expression.

The priest interrupted, "Corporal Olivetti, I sense that you are very dismayed with Duccio's behavior, but…"

Olivetti finally had an ear for the hostility that had consumed him for the past twenty two years, and he wasn't about to quit until he really was done. "Finally… And I mean finally…Duccio paid off those fines. But then just last December he was called back to court. This time he was being fined for not being present for mustering in other militia over the years at three other *contrade*. The man just kept moving and moving. Who does that in Siena? Has the man no loyalty?"

Olivetti walked towards the priest to make his final points at a closer distance, but in so doing he tripped over the small wooden object in the middle of the floor and lunged onto Father Giacobi's lap.

"*Scusi, scusi,*" the corporal said, "I am so embarrassed, I…"

Looking down at Olivetti's tattered dark blue military hat now sitting on his lap over the old man's head, the priest said, "Don't be embarrassed, but …what was that you tripped on, good Corporal? I thought I saw something lying on the floor."

First, getting down on his knees and then creaking to a more upright position, Olivetti answered breathlessly, "Oh, just an old toy from my youth…"

Speaking in a soft, measured voice, the priest said, "Dear Corporal, please, please sit down again and try to calm yourself. I don't want you to become ill over Duccio."

After he slowly lowered himself onto his chair again, Olivetti responded, "Don't worry, Father, I have been living for the opportunity to do something about that man. I just have to say one more thing. If it wouldn't have been for me being the one to talk with the magistrates over and over again about how Duccio avoided militia duty in his new *contrade* as well as my *contrada*... well…justice would never have been done."

"I guess that is something to be admired," Father Giacobi said softly with his emphasis on "guess." After pausing for a bit and shaking his head, the priest continued, "You and I have different reasons for our feelings, but we both believe that Duccio is not doing what is right. I don't want to see harm come to the man, but perhaps…and I say perhaps…we can work together to show how unworthy of elevation is Duccio's artwork."

Olivetti said, "But, with all due respect, Father, you saw how the people adored the Maestà."

"*Certo*, I agree with you, Corporal. Let the people have the front of the altarpiece, even though some of it may not be reverent enough. But the back of the altarpiece is what I object to. If we could somehow call Duccio's character into question and I could make a case with the magistrates about the fact that St. Peter may be lamenting in heaven to know how Duccio has used the face of Giovanni, the rag seller, to depict him…well, maybe just maybe, the magistrates and church officials would consent to my plan…and the people would not be too angry."

"And what would your plan be, Father?"

"I would propose two possibilities. One would be to move the altar to the back of the church so only its front could be seen. The other would be to paint over the back with black paint or drape a black cloth over that side."

The corners of Olivetti's lips crept up, and he said, "If we can prove that Duccio has poor morals, it is possible you could convince them the back of the altarpiece shows just that…in some ways."

As he fingered the crucifix around his neck, Father Giacobi added, "But whatever we come up with must be true. A man of my position cannot be a liar. And I don't want to see Duccio hurt too badly …" he continued as he stared at Olivetti. "We just have to come up with enough evidence that Duccio sometimes shows poor judgment."

The two men talked and talked until Olivetti told the priest about something he had observed that could be damaging to Duccio's reputation. When he heard the specifics of what Olivetti had observed, the priest agreed with the corporal that they had information that could look bad—but not too bad—for Duccio in the public's eyes. The story they would make known to the public had something to do with painting and a girl but not with sex.

⁂

At least Father Giacobi didn't want this to have to do with sex. Corporal Olivetti felt that the more despicable they could portray Duccio's behavior the more likely it would be that the people would condemn him.

To Corporal Olivetti everything was black or white: either you obeyed orders and did the right thing or you disobeyed orders and did the wrong thing. People who obeyed deserved to be rewarded, and those who disobeyed deserved to be punished.

Olivetti's first name was Alessandro. His father---Vincenzo--- had been a corporal also. Alessandro was raised by his father as well as a couple of aunts who lived together in the same tower. Unfortunately, his mother died in the process of giving birth to Alessandro.

To put food on the table for his son and himself, Vincenzo worked as a blacksmith and served as a corporal for the *Contrada* of *San Donato*. Vincenzo was angry at the world, because his wife had been taken from him at such a young age, and he could not find anyone else who would have him as a husband. So, he put his whole heart, soul, and animosity into being the boss of a small band of Sienese troops from his *contrada*.

As a result, all that Alessandro was exposed to was an emphasis on the military and doing the proper thing. His aunts had many children of their own and, even though they took care of Alessandro's physical needs when his father was working, they didn't give the time for a hug or a kiss for little Alessandro. The toy on which the aged Alessandro tripped was the one token of the few lighthearted childhood moments that the corporal still cherished.

Alessandro received recognition---which he interpreted as love---from his father when he helped shine his father's military boots or imitated him by saluting and enacting soldier-like games around the house.

When he was ten years old, Alessandro had asked, "Father, when I grow up, could I be a corporal just like you?"

"That could be, son. But you need to start calling me sir, if you want to be a real soldier."

"Yes, fath…yes sir, I will do that."

His father continued, "Most men have a regular job in addition to their corporal position. What else would you like to do, Alessandro?"

"Fath…sir I mean, I don't want to do anything else. I just want to be a corporal."

For the next few years, Vincenzo tried to get his son to consider an additional occupation. Seeing as how Alessandro liked to make sure that his clothes and shoes were always clean, his father suggested that perhaps he would like to be a tailor or a shoemaker someday. However, Alessandro was adamant; he would not consider any other career outside of the military.

While in the process of shining his boots, Vincenzo called Alessandro to his side one day. "Since serving in our *contrada* militia is the only thing of importance to you, my son, you may begin serving under me next year when you turn fifteen. With time, if you prove to me that you are a good soldier and hopefully a good leader of men, I will turn over my post as corporal to you, and I will just do my blacksmithing. I am starting to get old, Alessandro, and having two jobs is becoming too much for me."

Alessandro let out a loud, *"Magnifico!"*

"The only problem, son, is that you will not have much money if you only have your militia wages. Since you have insisted that being a corporal is the only thing you want, I have instructed my sisters that someday when I die, if you are not married, they should let you stay on one floor of the family tower."

"*Molte grazie*, sir," Alessandro said as he clicked his heels together and saluted. "I will make you proud. I will be a perfect soldier and, if you see fit to make me a corporal, I will make sure that every man in our *contrada* serves and…and…gives his best."

Six years later when Alessandro gained his much-desired post of corporal, the men serving under him talked behind his back: "How many afternoons a month do we have to come out to do these drills? This corporal is *pazzo* (insane)!" Nevertheless, most of the men dragged themselves to the drills for fear of being penalized or letting down the *contrada*. There was one man, though, whom Olivetti couldn't get under his grip no matter how hard he tried---Duccio di Buoninsegna.

And so, by virtue of his upbringing and character, Corporal Olivetti experienced no inner conflict when he conspired with Father Giacobi to make Duccio look bad in people's eyes. Alessandro's whole life---except for that little toy with which he actually still played----had centered on the military and making his men obey their commands. When he was a younger man, he rarely let it enter his mind that if he found a wife or even a friend it might fill the softer side of his heart. Wreaking revenge on Duccio was all he had left.

On the other hand, Father Giacobi felt more than a little twinge of guilt after the two men conspired together.

Giacobi had five brothers and sisters. His father, Luca, was a well-respected laborer and manager of a vineyard on the outskirts of Siena. Giacobi's mother, Rosa, was a warm, affectionate woman who wished that she could have learned to read and write. The only real opportunity for a girl to get an education was to enter a convent, and then the education would simply be used to copy manuscripts written by others. Rosa had too much of a spirit of adventure to be satisfied with being shut away from the world in a convent--- even though she would learn to read and write there.

One evening while they were sitting in front of their little *casa* as the six little ones slept, Luca and Rosa discussed their children.

Gazing up at the stars, Luca said, "Giacobi is so different from our other *bambini*, isn't he, *Mamma?*"

"What do you mean?"

"Today when they were done with their jobs, all of the *bambini* except for Giacobi started racing each other. They wanted to see who could be first to get from the vat where we stomp the grapes to that ladder the little ones prop against the trees to pick grapes."

"And so?"

"Giacobi didn't join in. He kept calling them, "Be careful. You'll trip. You'll fall on a bed of thorns.""

"*Si*, Luca, I too notice an extreme *prudenza* in our eldest. He was always like that. Do you remember how long it took him to walk by himself? He held on so tight to everything around him. He was so afraid of falling."

"*Si*, Rosa, but he is also extremely *intelligente.*"

"That is true, Luca. You know how I love to tell the children stories at night. Well, Giacobi always listens the most and asks good questions about everything that happens."

Luca added, "And when I give Giacobi instructions as to what to do while working in he fields, he always remembers what I say and follows my directions *perfettamente.*"

"Each one of our *bambini* is so different…" Rosa's voice trailed off into the starry night.

By the time Giacobi grew from little *bambino* to big boy of fourteen years of age, Giacobi and his parents decided it was time for him to figure out what path his life should follow. One evening Luca and Rosa shooed away the younger children and sat with Giacobi at the large table that Luca had once fashioned from a nearby fallen cypress tree.

Luca began, "Your mother and I have been talking about what you could do someday to support yourself and a family. You could be apprenticed in Siena if you have an interest in any of the guilds---leather working, painting, carpentry, blacksmithing, or whatever. Or…" Luca smiled and looked deeply into Giacobi's deep brown eyes, "you would be welcome to remain here in the country to work in the fields and perhaps…just perhaps…take over my job as supervisor of the vineyard. You are a very smart boy, and I think you could do that."

"Or," Giacobi brought up another possibility, "I could become a…a… priest." He fiddled with a piece of string in his hand and said, "I have been thinking about that for awhile, *Papà* and *Mamma*. I just love hearing about God in the little church near our vineyard, but, to tell you the truth, I love it even more when on the holidays we go into Siena and worship at the Cathedral."

Tears started rolling from Rosa's eyes, and she was quiet for a moment until she said, "I have noticed how you try to chant right along with the priests in Latin even if you don't know what it means."

"I was afraid to tell you how I feel about possibly becoming a priest, *Mamma*, because of those teardrops you are shedding. The only thing that would make me sad about being a priest would be…would be leaving you and *Papà* and my brothers and sisters."

Luca cleared his throat and said, "That's all right, son. Your mother and I will think about it. Go to bed now so you can be rested for tomorrow's picking."

"Si, *Papà. Buona notte, Mamma* and *Papà.*" Giacobi stood up and gave his mother an unexpected kiss on her forehead as he left.

That night under the stars again Luca and Rosa discussed their eldest. They agreed that he appreciated the religious side of life and that he probably would not mind being cooped up in a monastery for awhile since, unlike his mother, he was not the adventurous type. He would receive a marvelous education in the monastery, and he had the intelligence for it. Also, as a priest, he could use his education, if he so desired, to celebrate mass at church and give sermons.

Considering all of these things, Giacobi's parents could see that becoming a priest might be a good vocation for their first son.

The next day, his father made an announcement to Giacobi when they were out in the fields: "Your mother and I have decided that we will go along your plan to become a priest." Then he bent down just the little he needed to be eye level with his son, gave him a hug and said, "But we will miss you with all our heart if you enter the monastery as you would have to do."

That night Giacobi's mother brought him outside after the sun went down and the younger children were getting ready for bed. "You know how much I will miss you, but I want to give you a little advice to send you off. Here, have a seat with me on this bench, and listen to my words. You are an intelligent, serious-minded boy, Giacobi. That is good. However, you are a very careful boy, and you try to do everything just right. Sometimes that could lead to problems. Not everyone else will have your way of looking at things. My son, if you do go through all of the steps to become a priest, please try not to expect too much of yourself or others. While your job as a priest may be to help people do their best, there will be many times when your flock and you yourself will fall short…" Rosa struggled for a while, trying to put her thoughts into words, "And then you will need to accept rather than expect." With soft eyes and a tender touch to his hand, Rosa said, "Do you understand me, my dear Giacobi?"

"Si, *Mamma*," Giacobi said, but his flat tone lacked conviction.

We will see, Rosa thought, *we will see.*

His mother's words haunted the priest twenty years later on the night that he had the fateful meeting with Olivetti. On the one hand, Father Giacobi felt like maybe he was being too prudent and that he should just accept Duccio's new way of depicting Jesus and his followers; but then on the other hand, he felt that, as a priest, he had to uphold the time-honored religious tradition of depicting Jesus and his followers in an elevated, larger-than-life manner.

I wish I was at peace… but I am so filled with uncertainty. Perhaps this deciding right from wrong, good from bad is the greatest struggle for all human beings… it's just that I have been so locked away from a life of choices that I haven't had to make any difficult decisions.

And so on the night of their meeting, the corporal slept like a baby, but the priest tossed and turned ceaselessly.

CHAPTER 5

JUNE 12, 1311

Duccio was clicking a stick of drawing charcoal against his pewter mug as once again he was contemplating what to do with his apprentice, Elisabetta, who had been so helpful but could be a problem for him now. Then, all of a sudden the room grew dark even though it was early afternoon. The sun had been shining brightly, and there was no sense of rain in the air. Duccio looked out the openings where the shutters were pulled back and sensed that disaster was approaching. Immediately he threw down his piece of charcoal and scrambled out of the workshop.

The artist ran as fast as his fifty seven year old legs could take him. He hurried down his street---the *Via Stalloreggi*---and then down the *Via di Città*. Then he went up the *Via di Città* until it took him to the *Civetta Contrada* behind the Piazza del Campo. As the sky grew darker, the people on the streets were looking to the heavens to see what was happening. Others were rushing to get inside of their homes. Duccio would not allow himself to be distracted by the confusion around him. Once he reached his destination, Duccio dashed behind the tower that his son and pregnant daughter-in-law inhabited. While gazing up to the sky, Rafaella, his daughter-in-law, was outside throwing corn kernels from her apron pockets to the chickens in their yard. Duccio grabbed her by the shoulder and rushed her into the house.

"What are you doing, my father-in-law? Don't you see I am with child? You could have hurt me."

"Oh, no," Duccio said, although it was difficult for him to get out any words between his deep breaths. "On the contrary, I have saved you."

Rafaella looked at him with an open mouth and wide eyes, but soon neither of them could see each other.

"What is going on?" Rafaella asked.

"A couple of times in one's lifetime a person will experience this. Something has slowly moved in front of the sun. We don't know what it is, but it is an orb of some kind."

Shaking slightly, Rafaella asked, "Will it stay dark like this?"

"It will not remain for long like this."

"But why have you run all of the way over here to drag me into my home?"

"I must explain, Rafaella. If a pregnant woman remains outside when the orb is fully blocking the sun, she will have a baby with some kind of… deformity."

"*Ach*! …but how do you know?"

"I learned all of this from my uncle Alfonso when he was alive. Do you remember him?"

"Oh, yes, of course, the sweet man who somehow ate without a tooth left in his mouth."

"That's him. When I was a child, he often came to our home, and he would tell me about certain happenings that were omens of possible bad things that would happen in the future….unless…well…unless people took precautions."

"Precautions? Like what?"

"Like going inside your house if you are pregnant and you see an orb starting to go in front of the sun."

"What proof do you have that this is true, *Signor* Duccio?"

"Due to learning from Uncle Alfonso, I warned Taviana to go inside when she was pregnant and an orb was crossing the sun. Our baby was fine, but the neighbor's wife remained outside and gave birth to a boy with an unusually short arm. He was a great child and learned how to use both arms but still..."

"Well, then I thank you for dragging me into my house, my dear father-in-law."

Finally gathering enough strength to speak more boldly, Duccio added, "I made sure I came to rescue you for another reason. I felt I didn't try hard enough to save Tommè. You remember my dearly departed son, Tommè..."

"Oh, yes, *Dio mio,* his accident was so sad."

"Two days before he fell off of the roof Tommè had laughingly told me that a black cat had crossed his path. He had said that I would probably take that omen of possible harm very seriously, because I believed what that "silly old Alfonso had told me"--- to use the words of Tommè."

I shook my head and said, "Tommè, that was an omen that something terrible could happen to you. Please heed it, and be very careful in the next few days in whatever you do so no harm will befall you."

He said to me, "And you're the man who paints pictures of the Blessed Virgin and Baby Jesus? Do you remember how your own mother used to say you were foolish to listen to Uncle Alfonso?"

Duccio continued explaining to Rafaella, "My dearly departed mother always chided me for listening to her brother. I felt unable to express that having faith in God doesn't have to exclude heeding omens. Two days later... probably due to not being quite careful enough...you know how Tommè fell to his death on the way down the roof from cleaning a chimney."

"*Terribile, terribile.* Thank you for warning me, *Papà.* I really do appreciate it now that I have heard this story." Rafaella paused for a moment and then said, "but now I see that the light is returning."

"*Bene, bene.* But do you mind if I tell you of an omen that occurred to me on the day of the installation of the Maestà and how it worries me?"

"*Sì, sì*, sit down at our table, and tell me."

"I pricked my finger on the oxcart when the men were bringing the Maestà into the Cathedral. I got a splinter even. It took a couple of days to get it out."

"And why do you think that was a bad omen, *Papà?*"

"This has another thing to do with Uncle Alfonso's knowledge. He told me that if you prick your finger it could be a bad omen."

"And why would that be?"

"He said that it went back to the days of the prophet Daniel. He was working for a king who told Daniel to interpret some writing on a wall. Now this was a scary kind of writing on the wall. The king had just been sitting around and, all of a sudden, a finger appeared and wrote something on his wall. It was with great reluctance that Daniel shared his interpretation with the king, because Daniel said that it meant that the king's fortune would be taken from him. According to Uncle Alfonso…and the Bible…that very night enemies attacked and the king's life as well as his fortune was taken from him."

"All right… so what does that mean?"

"Whenever a person injures his finger, it means that bad luck can follow."

"So, you think, *Papà*, that because you got that splinter on the day of the installation of our beloved Maestà that evil could befall you?"

"*Sì*, I do."

"Well then, just be careful, *Papà*, because now you've almost got me convinced about these omens."

PART TWO

MARCH 7-27, 1311

FOUR MONTHS BEFORE THE INSTALLATION

CHAPTER 6

MARCH 7, 1311

With the creation of the Maestà coming to a close, Duccio wrestled with some difficult decisions about what to do with Elisabetta. Actually, Duccio got into the habit of thinking of her as his "half-man." That was because she had posed for so long as a boy in his workshop.

Unbeknownst to Duccio, he had first encountered Elisabetta in 1302---a full nine years earlier--- at the unveiling of his small Maestà panel at the newly constructed Palazzo Pubblico. It was just a small group of people who had come that day. Aside from Taviana and a couple of family members, Duccio only recognized his least favorite corporal and a priest from the Siena Cathedral.

Duccio had left the site of the installation for a while to go down the hall to look at some of the new building's intricately carved wooden doors and paneling. When he returned, he walked over to the Maestà and slightly adjusted its position on the podium. While doing so, he noticed a small family next to him. He caught sight of paint on the boy's hands and tunic and nodded to his fellow young artist with a smile. Just as he was about to look away, he saw that the girl in the family had paint-stained hands also. That was odd to Duccio, because girls and women just didn't paint. However, Duccio gave this observation no further thought at the time. Little did he know that the girl with the paint-stained hands would embark on a plan that ultimately would change his life forever---for better and worse.

On that fateful day in 1302, Elisabetta and her brother Tommaso had requested of their parents that they bring them to the Palazzo to see Duccio's work, because they loved his stained glass window at the cathedral and the artist to whom Tommaso apprenticed had claimed that Duccio's latest creation would be especially *meraviglioso*. On the way home from viewing the small Maestà, Elisabetta could not stop talking about the piece. Her father said, "Betta, please conduct yourself as a good Sienese girl. Walk and talk quietly, as you see your mother doing."

Elisabetta maintained a silent demeanor until they arrived home.

However, as soon as she set foot in the house, the words came tumbling out, "I want to paint, and I want to paint for *Signor* Duccio! *Mamma* and *Papà*, you see how much I like to work with pigments and brushes when Tommaso sneaks them home for me."

"We should have never let that start. Look what it has led to!" said *Mamma*.

"I can't help it, *Mamma*. You remember how as a child I loved looking at that stained glass window that *Signor* Duccio designed for the cathedral."

Her father laughed a little. "Yes, a couple of times you even cried when we tried to get you to quit staring at it and come home after mass."

"It's just something inside of me that wants to take an object or something that happened or a person and make it... last... with just a few pigments...and I want to make it beautiful just like *Signor* Duccio does."

"Oh, don't get so dramatic, Betta. You will never get close to being as good as *Signor* Duccio. Anyway, to me painting is just a job...a challenging job at that. I don't know why you get so carried away by it," said Tommaso.

"You just don't understand!" Betta jutted out her chin. "I just admire so much how *Signor* Duccio could paint on that small panel so many of the characters so perfectly. How could he have such a steady hand and be able to outline their features so well and then shade their faces so that they looked so real? I have never seen anything like that."

"You do have a point, Betta," her father said. "I have done carpentry work for a lot of the churches in the various *contrade*, and I am used to seeing a different type of painting. How do I describe it? The characters are flat and large...they are impressive, but a little...a little...frightening also."

Elisabetta continued, "And the colors, *Papà*, have you ever seen such brilliant colors in the other church paintings in Siena?"

"I must admit that I haven't seen any colors as bright as Duccio's. I have seen some of the other painters put gold in like Duccio did in this Maestà. But their gold work looks...how shall I say it... dull next to Duccio's."

"I want to be a part of what *Signor* Duccio is doing!" insisted Elisabetta.

Her mother tried to change the subject and ordered Elisabetta to help her cut some vegetables for a stew and then sweep the floor. Her father and brother looked at each other and bolted down the stairs to get involved in some carpentry project---any carpentry project.

However, Elisabetta harangued her family for two long weeks, until her parents finally relented. While Elisabetta was washing out a pot after a family dinner, her mother said, "Your father and I have agreed that if you feel you need so much to try to talk with *Signor* Duccio, you can go. But he and I will not be a part of this. You will have to go with your brother, since he is an artist's apprentice himself."

Elisabetta jumped up and down and hugged her mother.

Her brother said, "What? Why must I go with Betta? This is so foolish for a girl to do."

"Yes, you must, Tommaso and...and... there will be a reward if you do it," Betta said.

"Oh, I'm sure it would be some reward," Tommaso harrumphed.

On the very next morning as she lay snuggled in her woolen cover, Betta heard her mother call, "Betta, Betta, wake up!"

"What? What?"

"You begged me to get you up soon after the sun came up so you could get ready to see *Signor Duccio*."

"Oh, yes, *Mamma, grazie* for waking me up. Tommaso, get up! We don't have long before we have to get going!"

"This is *ridicolo, ridicolo!*" Tommaso yelled as he rolled over and tried to get one more wink.

But Elisabetta was not allowing that. She went over to her brother, shook him and said, "We must get going."

"I told you…I told you…you owe me big for this."

"Let me think…hmm…how about if I go----instead of you---to help *Papà* this Saturday when he goes outside the city walls to chop down a tree for one of his projects? You can sleep then as late as *Mamma* will allow you."

"All right, all right," Tommaso shrugged as they both went to the kitchen table where their mother sliced a couple of huge pieces of bread from a loaf and handed one to each with a mug of ale. She said to Elisabetta, "I know you hate to drink ale…especially in the morning, my daughter…but it seems like we will never get clean water like the Florentines have."

Sitting down at the table and answering with a smile, Elisabetta said, "I don't care what I eat or drink today as long as I get to see *Signor* Duccio."

"Why do you think that the great Duccio will listen to a twelve year old girl like you…and… and how can a girl be an apprentice?"

"I have a plan, *Mamma*, don't worry."

"And those clothes you are wearing. Your worn-out, everyday tunic and leggings with your brother's old boots. Couldn't you at least wear your dress and your own shoes?"

"It's all part of the plan, *Mamma*, all part of the plan," Elisabetta responded as she pulled Tommaso by the arm to scurry out of the house and down the streets to go to Duccio's workshop…the location of which Tommaso had discovered through the artist for whom he apprenticed.

The truth was that Elisabetta's mother secretly admired her daughter's courage, and that is why she heeded her request to be awakened earlier than usual. As Anna prepared to go to mass and then the market, she prayed, *Holy Mother of God, please help all of this turn out for good.*

On their long, hasty walk to Duccio's workshop, Tommaso complained, "I hope I am not late to work now. You might get hired as an apprentice, but I might lose my own apprenticeship in the process."

Elisabetta struggled to hurry despite wearing the over-sized boots. However, she had enough breath to respond, "You know this is why I wanted us to get up early…so that you could still make it to work on time after we get to talk to *Signor* Duccio."

"Yeah, hopefully I will make it in time," said Tommaso as he dodged worshippers scurrying in the opposite direction to get to mass.

Eventually Duccio's workshop was in sight. The girl pulled her hood over her forehead and whispered, "There is one of Duccio's assistants laying out small articles for sale. He is the one you can ask for an audience with Duccio. First, we can pretend like we're looking to buy something."

"All right, all right," Tommaso murmured, and then they walked up to the stand with book covers, crucifixes, and miniature Madonna paintings. Tommaso asked of the apprentice, "Kind sir, could we possibly see the most honored *Signor* Duccio to ask of him a brief question?"

Smiling with the enjoyment of being called "sir," Mimmo, the apprentice, stepped into the workshop and then into Duccio's office to inquire as to whether he could speak with a couple of visitors.

"I am not too busy, Mimmo. You may show them into my office."

And so began Duccio's nine year relationship with Elisabetta Buccini.

Duccio recalled almost everything from his first conversation with Elisabetta and her brother, because a monumental decision finally evolved from this initial meeting.

Tommaso had pointed to his sibling and said, "Please forgive us, *Signor* Duccio, but she begged me to bring her here to see you. I told her that you are "the great one" in Siena and we are not worthy to visit you, but she... she... implored me to escort her here."

Duccio remembered how he smiled a little as he looked at Elisabetta and said, "I thought you were a "he" and not a "she," but anyhow, my child, why do you wish so much to see me?"

Elisabetta stuttered and stammered, and so her brother explained: "I suppose you don't remember seeing us when you were adjusting your Maestà on its stand at the Palazzo a couple of weeks ago, but my sister was...how shall I say it...astounded...yes astounded by your work."

Duccio looked at her and asked, "What exactly did you like about my painting?"

Elisabetta finally answered in a quiet tone, "*Signore*, I loved the way you made the Holy Virgin looks so sweet and human. Also, I admired how you painted the people to look so real and... detailed, I guess you could say."

Duccio noticed that she looked more directly at him as she continued to speak, "And the blues, the greens and the reds were so bold and pure. Then ...then... there was this bright glow on everything...I think from your flecks of gold?" she asked.

"You have an artistic eye, young lady," Duccio said, as he remembered feeling complimented by her words even though she was such a young person.

"I must admit that I am a secret painter myself, *Signor* Duccio," Elisabetta had continued as she pulled her hood over her forehead further. And then she described what she called her "crimes" of encouraging Tommaso to smuggle home a couple of brushes and then tiny supplies of pigments in the seashells in which the apprentices mixed their colors.

"With my art supplies and scraps of wood from my father's carpentry shop, I have painted a few small pictures. One I brought to show you today..."

At that moment, she had pulled out a small painting on wood from beneath her tunic.

Before she turned it over to show to him, Elisabetta apologized, "I know this may not be good work and that I have a lot to learn, but I had my father stand for awhile as a model, and I came up with this...this vision...of St. John...he... he's preaching in the wilderness."

When she finally revealed her painting, Duccio remembered how amazed he was. "*Magnifico!*" he responded.

Elisabetta blushed as she revealed her proposed plan. "Good sir, if I would wear a boy's tunic everyday to work and pretend like I couldn't speak, could you take me into your workshop? No other apprentices need to know that I am a girl."

Silence filled the room, and it remained until Elisabetta swept it away.

"All I would ask of you is a small lunch everyday to sustain me, and in return I would do whatever job you would require. I will prepare the wooden surfaces, mix pigments for you, go to the market to buy supplies...whatever you need. I just want to be a part of what you are creating, and I need...I want...to learn how to paint... like you do...inasmuch as I possibly can." She hesitated and quietly added, "It is all I can think about."

A lump had formed in Duccio's throat. The girl was asking a lot. It was completely against all of society's customs and traditions for a woman to paint...unless the woman was an apprentice to an artist because she was a widow and needed the *soldi* to provide for her family.

Inner conflict had assaulted him, though, because Duccio knew what a passion it was for him to create art. Even though the planning and execution of his work devoured most of his thoughts and emotions, he knew he could not live without it.

Duccio responded tersely, "I will have to think about this. Leave your work with me for a couple of weeks. Then come back, and I will give you my answer."

CHAPTER 7

MARCH 21, 1311

Duccio could not turn Elisabetta away.

When she came back, Duccio had explained to her, "I will give you the boy's name Paolo which means small. You have good luck in that the two main apprentices I have now…and probably will continue to have for some time… are rather silly boys….greatly talented…but loving to joke around with each other constantly. They will probably not bother you unless you draw attention to yourself. My other apprentice, Mimmo, who you saw selling my wares outside to travelers, is a rather simple young man with a heart of gold who would not harm a flea and would probably never guess our little secret. I will tell the lads to call you Paolo but that you are mute and unable to speak… so…please, continue to wear your baggy clothes and keep your lips sealed."

Elisabetta came close to hugging Duccio and accepted his terms with delight.

Within a couple of months, the apprentice Paolo had demonstrated how she could contribute to the workshop. Gilding with gold was one of the ways. She had such small, steady fingers that she applied the slivers of gold ever so accurately to the areas that Duccio specified.

And when it came to Paolo's mixing of colors, Duccio could hardly suppress an occasional *"Fantastico"* or *"Perfetto."* Although Duccio gave birth to the original hues for the robes, skin tones, buildings, and hundreds of other details to be painted, his new apprentice Paolo learned quickly, and she magically recreated Duccio's tints with the colored powders and egg yolks to come up with a perfect match when needed. Particularly impressive was how Paolo could use a mortar and pestle and take the lapus lazuli blue stone Duccio had bought from Eastern merchants to transform it into the perfect ultramarine that Duccio wanted for Mary's robe.

And how could Duccio forget the fact that Paolo had brought her father into the picture just when his skills were needed? One afternoon Duccio was muttering to his apprentices---Simone and Ambrogio---that he couldn't find a good carpenter to help him break down and then reassemble his sixteen by fifteen foot Maestà for the trip to the cathedral.

Paolo had overheard what Duccio said. She spoke quietly with him in his office when he was alone.

"If I may have a word with you, *Signor* Duccio, I would like to share something with you."

"Yes," Duccio said, "What is on your mind?"

In a whisper, she said, "My father is a master carpenter and could possibly help you with your problem."

"*Interessante*, send your father to me someday soon, and I will discuss the matter with him."

Upon discussing his conundrum with Paolo's father, Duccio was impressed with the carpenter's suggestions. Duccio went to The Council of Nine and asked for more *soldi* to pay the wages of Arnolfino, the carpenter. However, they warned that the cost of the Maestà was exceeding their budget, and he might have to let go of two of his apprentices whose wages were now being paid by the Council.

Duccio had shoved these financial warnings to the back of his mind and concentrated instead on working with Arnolfino to complete the final assembly issues.

And, then just recently, Paolo had helped Duccio even if it was somewhat against her will. It had to do with the angels. The perfect face for his angels had eluded him.

Alone in his office, Duccio had prayed, *Dio mio, please help me find a suitable subject for my angels.*

Ambrogio and Simone had done an exceptional job of sketching subjects from the Commune for all of the other figures in the Maestà's religious drama. The only face that they couldn't get right was that of the angels. Duccio had wanted all of the angels to have the same face. So, he only needed one suitable model for the expression he wanted to capture.

When Duccio reminded the apprentices that time was almost up, and they had to get the right angel face soon, Simone replied, "Master, we have tried to find the face of a young, innocent girl with a look of compassion for others--- just as you have ordered. How about that face of Anna, the baker's daughter, or Giovanna, the blacksmith's wife?"

"No, no. They are beautiful women, but they don't look like they care enough for others."

"Why are you struggling so much over this one face, *Signore*?" asked Ambrogio.

"This won't just be one face, Ambrogio. I want each of the nineteen angels to have the same face. I'll put slightly different necklaces and robes on each one, but I'll tell you two reasons for why I want all of the angels to be basically the same."

Duccio pointed at the panel painting. "See all of the people in this picture so far. I tried to make each one different---each with his or her own clothing, face, hair, and symbol to explain exactly who each one is. Right?"

"*Corretto*," said the apprentices in unison.

"As a result, there is a lot happening in the painting. The viewer's eye can hardly take in all the detail. You see where I have done a simple outline in charcoal of where each angel will go. If their faces and bodies are all basically the same, there will be a sameness and regularity to keep the worshippers from feeling overwhelmed."

"*Sì, sì*," the young men said.

"And have I shared with you yet why I want the angels to be not just beautiful but also compassionate?

They shook their heads "no."

"Because I want worshippers to know that if they believe, God will send such loving angels to watch over them too with the love and kindness they are radiating to Mary and Jesus."

"Hmm," said Simone, "the angels in other Maestàs I have seen look more like... like mannequins...that I see at my tailor's shop when I shop for my fine attire."

"You and your fine attire, Simone," said Duccio with a half smile, "but you're absolutely *corretto* and I have a belief...I believe that this has led to more prayers said out of ritual rather than...how shall I say it...true communion with God. I want to change that."

After pausing for a while, Duccio said, "Tomorrow, I want the two of you, Ambrogio and Simone, to go out again and look for my perfect, loving angel face."

Duccio added, "Now everyone back to work. Mimmo, how many more coats of *gesso* do you still have to put on that piece of poplar for my painting of the Crucifixion scene?"

"Just one more, Master," responded Mimmo as he quit eavesdropping and went back to the table where he was applying the glue with small cloths.

"Good, and, Paolo, do we have enough slivers of gold leaf to adequately finish the gold on Mary's robe?"

Turning to obtain Paolo's response, Duccio looked at her straight in the eyes for a change. Her hood had fallen back a little, and Duccio took a deep breath.

He remembered that moment distinctly.

During the rest of the day, Duccio shot stares towards Paolo with his light-beam eyes. To avoid his gaze, Paolo moved her head a little or adjusted the angle at which she sat--- but to no avail.

A short while before the usual end of the workday, Duccio told the other apprentices that they could go home early, but he asked Paolo to stay. Ever the teasers, Ambrogio and Simone whispered to Paolo, "Trouble, trouble." Of course, Paolo did not say a word.

With a wide grin, Duccio ushered Paolo into his office. As he steered her to the chair reserved for his most prominent patrons, Duccio put his hand on her shoulder, and she winced.

"Don't be afraid, Paolo, I just have a simple request of you."

The girl shook ever so slightly and waited.

"I would like you to be the subject for my angels."

"Oh," Paolo's gasp sounded more like one of relief than joy. "But I don't know if I could do that, *Signore*."

"When you heard me talking with Ambrogio and Simone about my need to find the perfect angel, you looked at me with such a kind, worried look that I knew you should be the subject for my nineteen angels."

Duccio remembered how Paolo had cringed. It did not look like she warmed to his idea.

Before she had a chance to say "no," he went on to add: "In payment, I will give you some painting supplies to take home. And so that you know this is strictly…well…business…I want you to know that I would discuss this with my dear wife, Taviana. If she does not want you to be my subject for the angels. I would…of course…respect her wishes."

"Master, how can we do this? What would the other apprentices think? To them I am a boy."

"This afternoon when I was studying you for the role of angel, I gave some thought to how this might work. You could stay just a little later for about four sessions after the other apprentices leave. They wouldn't even know you were staying on. Your brother could pick you up since the sun may be setting by the time we are done…"

"Oh, *Signore,* I don't know about this," Paolo tried to protest.

"But you see, Paolo, this will make the difference between the Maestà being a pretty altarpiece and…well… a soul-stirring work of art that will truly touch the hearts and minds of the people. *Per favore*, go home and consider this…seriously."

That night when he lay in bed with his wife Duccio had quietly whispered to Taviana, "I love you, my dear."

"Oh, Oh," she responded, "Have you gotten yourself in debt again or do you want me to make your favorite meal tomorrow?"

"Can I just tell you that I love you?

"I know you too well, *mio marito*. You want something."

"All right. Well, I do love you anyhow, but there does happen to be something on my mind."

Taviana sighed.

"I have been sending my apprentices out everyday to find the perfect subject for my nineteen identical angels. They have not found the face I want. So, lo and behold, I looked at that little apprentice of mine…"

"Oh, the little boy."

"Well, the little boy is actually a…a…girl."

Taviana's head jerked back in response. "A girl! Isn't it against some rule not to have a girl as an apprentice?'

"Actually, Taviana, I don't think there has ever been a written rule against having a female apprentices. It's more just a matter of custom not to have them."

Taviana mused for a while. She rehashed her feelings about how Duccio could cut quite a nice figure when he was clean-shaven and neatly dressed and about how those blue eyes of his could mesmerize a woman. But he was all business when it came to his art, and she knew Duccio loved her and their family above anyone else. Her instincts told Taviana to trust Duccio..

"All right, all right, I know you, *mio sposo*. And I know that when you get it fixed in your mind to do something, you can't let it go until the thing is accomplished."

Now just four months before the installation of his Maestà Duccio had a heavy heart when he thought about eventually letting go of Elisabetta. Within a day after his request to pose for his angels, Elisabetta had consented, and she had assisted him in so many other ways. However, someone would eventually discover that she was a female, and Corporal Olivetti and perhaps even Father Giacobi would delight in using this against him in some way.

The difficulty with letting her go was that he could not see a future for her or any other young woman in the art world. Nevertheless, Duccio told himself that this was not his problem. Years ago Elisabetta had begged him to take her on. He had done so. And she had learned how to paint, just as she wanted.

Selfishly, I know that I still need her for a couple of more sittings to capture her expression for the perfect angel, but eventually I will have to let go of her…. before it is too late.

CHAPTER 8

MARCH 24, 1311

On this day, Duccio kept Elisabetta unusually late, because he finally felt he was capturing her expression of true compassion, and he did not want to quit painting. The sun was setting, but Tommaso had somehow forgotten to come get his sister. Betta lied to Duccio that he was waiting outside, and she scurried home.

The church bells signaled that daylight was drawing to an end, and the city gates soon would be locked. All respectable Sienese women were inside or, if outside, they were with a male chaperone.

Corporal Olivetti, who was a neighbor of Betta's family, happened to be taking a walk to stretch his stiff legs. He saw a small person with a hooded body hurrying towards him in the shadows. Olivetti said to himself, *This person is up to no good.* At that very moment, he recognized it was the neighbor girl. He had seen her wearing that same old, faded orange tunic for the last eight years and had always envied the way she so quickly sped over the cobblestones.

Because the street was only about five feet wide, the Corporal could easily gain the girl's attention. "Young lady, I believe you are the carpenter's daughter…what are you doing out at this hour of night without a family member or chaperone?"

Startled, Elisabetta responded to the man whom her parents disliked because he always meddled in other people's business: "Good Corporal, I was just…I was just…"

"Explain yourself, young lady, we don't have all night."

"I was just at the market trying to buy some fresh meat for my family."

"Why couldn't your mother do that?"

"Oh well…well…everyone in my house is ill, so I had to go alone. I…I… lost track of time and didn't realize that the sun would be setting soon."

Olivetti commanded, "Take your hands from under your tunic and show me the fresh meat that you bought."

Without thinking, Elisabetta obeyed his command and showed him her hands.

"I couldn't buy anything, because…because… all of the fresh meat was purchased before I arrived."

Seeing paint on Elisabetta's hands, the Corporal bellowed, "And what is this on your hands? This is paint that an artist uses, and because the colors are so bold it looks as though you have been using them today. Why is that?"

Trying to keep coming up with excuses, Betta answered, "I was at the workshop where my brother apprentices and, since he is ill, I went to get his warm cloak that he left there yesterday. Also, I had to tell his master why he didn't come to work today."

"*Si,* and why would that lead to you having paint on your hands?"

"Oh, I happened to touch some shells that had paint around their edges as I was…as I was…looking for my brother's cloak."

"That all sounds very suspicious to me, young lady, and I don't know if I believe you. Just remember your place as a woman and do not bring disgrace upon our dearly loved *San Donato Contrada.* Do you understand?"

"*Si, si,* good Corporal, I will heed your words," Betta said as she walked as rapidly as she could to get home.

CHAPTER 9

MARCH 26, 1311

As he and Mimmo were closing the shutters and cleaning up after a hard day of painting, Duccio heard a loud thumping on his workshop door. It sounded like a demanding---perhaps foreboding---thumping. Duccio slowly went to answer.

A man in the uniform of a Sienese messenger spoke loudly, "Are you *Signor* Duccio di Buoninsegna?"

"*Si, si.*"

"Good sir, I have a message from the Council of Nine that I am delivering to you."

"*Grazie...*I guess," said Duccio under his breath.

The messenger clicked together his heels, saluted, and marched out of the workshop. Duccio breathed a sigh of relief. This was just one of the many correspondences he exchanged with the Council of Nine about the progress of the Maestà. It requested him to appear before the Council on the following morning to discuss finances.

⁂

On the next morning, Duccio proceeded to the Palazzo Pubblico. When he arrived, he was ushered as usual into the chambers of the Council of Nine.

The man who had headed the Maestà planning committee spoke, "*Signor* Duccio, how are you on this fine---although crisp--- morning?"

"*Bene, bene.*"

"And how is our Maestà progressing?"

"It couldn't be better, good sir. We will complete the altarpiece right on schedule."

"Well, *Signor* Duccio," the man continued, "We are...I am sorry to say again we are concerned about the costs. As you know, the cost of your gold has exceeded what we budgeted for it...and now... and now you need specialists to come in to do the varnishing, you've said."

Duccio slumped in his chair.

"You have perhaps noticed, *Signore,* that we have been putting stones on several of our streets that are still just dirt roads. Paying men to go out in the country to gather stones, cut them if necessary...well, you can imagine that this has been quite expensive. Although our Commune has been blessed with considerable wealth in the last couple of years, we cannot keep spending, spending..."

"So, what are you saying?" Duccio asked.

"We want you to let go two of your apprentices."

Duccio winced.

"As you know, I have come to see you on a couple of occasions to see how work was progressing, and I have struck up conversations with the lads you have working there...except for the mute one...God bless him."

Duccio felt blood rushing to his head.

"In conversing with your other apprentices, I have found that they have been with you for quite a number of years."

"But they are so valuable to me..."

"We know that you highly prize your gifted group, but now that we have to pay for the varnishers to come in and finish the project...well...we cannot afford to pay their salaries anymore. You will have to let two of them go."

"I don't like it, but... I understand," Duccio said. He stood up, slightly tipped his cap to the Council members and quietly said "*Buon giorno*," as he walked out of the meeting.

CHAPTER 10

MARCH 27, 1311

Dripping with slime from head to toe, the usually dapper Simone tumbled into the workshop cursing and swearing. Everyone rushed over to see what happened.

"*Dio mio*, I was running late for work…"

"Oh, and what's new about that?" Ambrogio chuckled.

"This time I was rushing down *Via* Granachi when I decided to cut through an alley. I'm running along and some *stupida signora* decides to dump a pail of greasy water from the third floor of her tower, and it landed right on my head."

Simone took off his crimson cap with its yellow feather and shook it to rid it of the muck. Ambrogio laughed loudly. Paolo struggled to hold back anything sounding like a giggle. Mimmo came up to Simone with a semi-clean rag and tried to wipe the dirty water off of Simone's clothing.

"And this is my favorite hat. The girls give me extra looks whenever I wear it," Simone said as he kept shaking it. "Thanks for your help, Mimmo... I could do without the snickers from you other two."

However, Simone knew he would laugh at his co-workers too if they ended up with this mess. So he wasn't really angry with them.

Duccio summoned the courage to talk to Simone. He came out of his office and said, "When you have made yourself handsome again...at least in your opinion...come to my office so that I may have a word with you."

"Trouble," Ambrogio whispered to Simone.

"I'm not worried," Simone shrugged.

A few moments later, Simone stepped into Duccio's office and said, "*Buon Giorno*, Master Duccio. You wish to speak with me?"

"*Sì,*" Duccio responded. He tried to be serious, but he could hardly squelch a smile gazing at the impeccably dressed Simone looking and smelling like a drenched rat. "How do I begin to recount how much you have learned and grown since you came here as a boy waiting for his first whisker? You have been..."

"Are you trying to get rid of me, *Signor* Duccio?"

"Well, if you must push for me to get to the point so quickly, yes."

"Is it because of my tendency to be late to work?"

"No, no, that has nothing to do with it. The Council of Nine is pushing me...I am so sorry to say...to get rid of two of my apprentices so that I can pay two varnishers to finish the Maestà... You've worked on this project long enough to know how they are always worried about the *soldi.*"

After about a minute of silence, Simone said, "*Sì, sì, Signor* Duccio, I understand."

Simone even smiled.

Duccio stared at him.

"You're taking this very well, Simone."

"You have taught me so much, *Signor* Duccio. But, to tell you the truth, I feel...I feel... ready to do some things on my own. You love doing great big paintings like the Maestà altarpiece, and I do too, but I also like doing smaller pictures..."

Duccio pointed to Simone's final project that was leaning against the wall and said. "I understand."

Since Simone had just completed the painting and they had not reviewed it together yet, Duccio took the opportunity to do so now. "Let's look together at your work here. I like the way you have put Mary into a type of…a type of… religious drama on an ornate stage."

Duccio gesticulated in turn to every aspect of the painting that he wanted to address. "Here you dress your subjects in fancy outfits and put them in lush landscapes with delicate flowers."

"Here you applied my left-over gold leaf to create a glistening backdrop for what I call…the…performers in your religious… drama."

"And here you have created perfectly round haloes with your superb compass work."

"All in all, your work reflects a love of the beautiful and ornate, and that is *magnifico*."

"You are definitely right, *Signor* Duccio."

"I have given your style some thought, Simone, and I think that your work will be appreciated by many who want to be entertained rather than frightened by a religious piece of art."

Simone lowered his head and quietly admitted: "*Grazie, grazie, Signore*, but I must admit that another artist has been talking with me about being his partner, but he didn't want to take me from your service… if you still needed me. You have probably heard of the fresco artist, Memmo di Filipuccio."

"*Sì,*" Duccio responded. "I have worked with Memmo myself a little. He is a fine artist, but a big talker…."

"That he is," agreed Simone. "He is doing a fresco in one of the churches in San Gimignano. He is coaxing both me and my brother Donato to join him in his undertaking."

"Well, this all comes as somewhat of a surprise…but I am happy for you. The successful completion of your master project entitles you to be an artist in your own right… Stay…if you wish…for a short while and observe the early stages of what the glazers will do, but I cannot afford to pay you for any more than two more weeks."

Then Duccio added, "But, please, come back on the day of the installation to help bring the Maestà to her final resting place."

"*Certamente, Signore*, I already have my outfit picked out for the big parade."

Duccio laughed, then stood up, shook Simone's hand, and said, "Thank you for your *eccellente* contributions to the Maestà, and remember you will always have a home and family here."

Simone replied with moist eyes, "Thank you too, *Signore*, for all you have taught me."

As Simone was walking towards the office door, he turned and whispered, "With all due respect, *Signor* Duccio…you never fooled Ambrogio and me about Paolo. We knew all along that she was a girl, but she has what you called… "the gift"…and we didn't want to hinder her from using it."

Duccio chuckled as he pretended to shove Simone out the door. "Get out of here now," he said.

Then Duccio heaved a deep sigh. He asked himself, *What is this sigh for? Is it a sigh of contentment or sadness?* He concluded that it was probably a little bit of both. He would miss this apprentice.

As soon as he collected himself from his talk with Simone, Duccio called in Ambrogio. He knew that the moment Simone left the office he would tell the other apprentices what happened. So as not to have Ambrogio feeling apprehensive about his fate all day, he wanted to have the conversation with him right away.

Upon entering Duccio's office, Ambrogio hung his head slightly. His usual smile was nowhere to be found.

Duccio said, "I imagine that Simone has spoken with you."

"*Si*, Master, he has, and I imagine that you will not require my services any longer either."

Duccio walked over to Ambrogio, put his arm over his shoulder, and brought him to the other side of the room where Ambrogio's master project---a large city scene---was leaning against one of the shop walls. As in Simone's case, Ambrogio had just finished his piece, and this was Duccio's first opportunity to review it with him.

"You have so much talent, Ambrogio. Look at your creation. You have captured human beings in motion. Look at these things," Duccio said as he pointed to each. "A boy riding a horse, a butcher selling a side of beef, a woman hanging out the laundry…all in perfect proportions."

Ambrogio smiled weakly and commented, "Yes, that's the kind of stuff I like to paint."

"And you have set all of them moving within our city streets. You have even captured a little of the landscape and the activities of the people outside of our city walls," Duccio said as he pointed to one side of the painting.

"*Si, Signor* Duccio, maybe it's a sin, but I don't like just creating religious art. I want to show common people in their everyday lives."

"That is not a sin, Ambrogio. Look here also at how you designed all of these intricate geometric borders to frame your scenes. *Bellissimo!*"

Ambrogio's chin went up when he looked at Duccio and listened to his comments.

"Also, Ambrogio, you have developed your own special hues for your type of art that makes everything look like real."

"With all due respect to you and the way you used such bright, bold colors in your Maestà, *Signor* Duccio, my type of art is different. When one looks around our fair city, one sees lots of shades of grays, browns, muted oranges and soft greens, and that is what I wanted to capture."

Duccio responded, "On the basis of this outstanding final project and your nine years of serving as one of my most gifted apprentices ever, I pronounce you "graduated" and ready to be called an artist in your own right!"

"*Molte grazie*, Master Duccio, but I…I…don't want to leave your workshop. Simone told me that you let him go and that you would probably let me go too. I felt…well… destroyed… when I heard the news."

Ambrogio started sobbing and shaking. "Where will I go? What will I do? And we are so close to finishing the Maestà. I want to be here for its march to the Cathedral."

Duccio put his arm on Ambrogio's shoulder again. "I want you to make that triumphant march with us to the Cathedral, and I will invite you back to do that. But I imagine that Simone explained how we had to cut back…"

"*Sì, Sì*, Simone explained it all to me." He hesitated as he cried, "I feel like I am still a boy, though. You have been like a father to me, *Signor* Duccio, and I am…I am afraid to go out on my own."

Suddenly an idea came to Duccio. "I'll tell you what, Ambrogio: How about if you use a small area of my workshop to do little jobs that are originally sent to me? I will ask the patrons if it is acceptable that I give the work to you as a fellow artist in my shop. These little jobs would be like painting *cassone* and archive covers, but…." Duccio was still thinking this through, "I would give you these jobs **only if** I am obtaining larger commissions… so that I can feed my family."

"*Bene, bene*, and *molte grazie*," said Ambrogio as he wiped away his tears.

"When you prove yourself by doing superior work on these commissions---as I know you can--- you will gain the reputation you need to start your own workshop."

Silence ensued, and then Ambrogio introduced a new subject. "Master, you remember my brother Pietro, don't you?"

"How could I forget him? He was one of my first apprentices about ten years before you came along. How is he doing?"

"He is very successful. I don't want to hurt your feelings, good Master, but Pietro likes Giotto's style. In the little time that we have talked in recent years, Pietro told me that he really appreciated what you taught him about making picture stories about the Bible and especially setting them right in a place like Siena. But what he really likes about Giotto is that he tries so hard to show… the emotions…the feelings… of Jesus' followers."

"Don't worry about offending me with that," Duccio responded. Feeling tired from standing and talking so intensely for what seemed like an hour, Duccio sat down at his desk chair and motioned Ambrogio to sit down on a stool nearby.

"Everyone has their own style, Ambrogio. Giotto has his, and I have mine, but we are both trying to take art to a new place."

Duccio paused for a few moments and then he said, "Why don't you consider working with your brother, Pietro?"

Ambrogio put his head down again and paused, "Pietro has always regarded me as kind of...how can I put it? Annoying...yes, an annoying younger brother. When we were children, I followed him everywhere. He was so good with a slingshot..." Ambrogio's voice trailed off, and he stared into space.

Then Ambrogio continued, "Now Pietro is married and lives in the Cegna *Contrada*---a long walk from where I live with our parents. He has six children and a wife who you could say doesn't appreciate me or anyone who takes Pietro's attention." He hesitated and then added, "But I can kind of see her point, since he is gone from home so much working in Florence...sometimes with Giotto."

For a little while, the younger and older artist sat together in silence.

Then Ambrogio rose.

"*Grazie* for listening and helping me, Master. I knew that this talk would come some day, but I didn't want to face it." Ambrogio was quiet for a moment and then said, "I will take you up on your offer to let me work in the corner of your shop while I try to hunt down Pietro and see if he will have me. *Grazie* again for all of your *eccellente* teaching and...and... for putting up with my silly ways."

Then Ambrogio lifted his cap, tipped it and said, "Have a good rest of the day, *Signor* Duccio, and thank you for helping me with this change."

⚜

Duccio sat at his desk, put his head in his hands, and took some deep breaths. *This has been quite a day*, he thought. But he had one more task to accomplish.

He went to the door and called, "Mimmo, could you come in?"

Mimmo quickly came to the door and then shuddered.

After Mimmo entered his office, Duccio began, "I hope that you are doing well today, Mimmo. You look pale."

"Oh, yes, *Signor* Duccio, I am doing fine," Mimmo replied without emotion.

"Well, I would like to talk with you about your future at my workshop." Mimmo's olive skin turned ghostly white.

"*Per favore*, don't worry. You have a future here."

Mimmo took the deepest breath he had ever breathed in his life.

"You have been my most reliable and probably hardest-working apprentice. You are always ready to help and give your very best… especially in laying down the gesso and doing the bole…two very messy jobs…"

Mimmo blurted out, "*Scusi, Signor* Duccio, I am not really good at art. I can't draw or paint, but I love working here and…for you. Our workshop is known in San Gimignano, Florence, and probably…probably even in Rome…"

Duccio interjected, "As long as I have the money to pay you a humble salary, you will have a place at this workshop…if you so desire. The way you clean the brushes, sweep the floor, set out the wares for sale…is invaluable to me…especially with your cheerful attitude and all."

"Oh, *Signore*, I am so glad that you appreciate my assistance. It is an honor for me to work for you.…To me, you are like…like…the king of painting in all of Siena!"

"You are too flattering, Mimmo, but that is all right. As I began to say, I would like to keep you on, but I will have to lower your *salario* just a little. The Council has required that I let go two of my apprentices, which, I am sure you know by now. That I have done, but I need an "assistant" like you to keep things organized around here. Will you continue with me in this way for as long as I can afford to pay you?"

Bowing slightly as he doffed his cap, Mimmo answered, "*Certamente*, good master, I will remain your loyal assistant for as long as you wish."

And that ended Duccio's difficult day. Duccio thought, *Elisabetta will have to wait to learn her fate. I don't want to be selfish, but all I have to pay for is her daily lunch. She is a big help to me, and I still need her to pose some more for my angels. I'll just have to take the risk of keeping her on for awhile longer.*

CHAPTER 11

MARCH 28, 1311

Corporal Olivetti was sitting on his old wooden chair. He considered playing with his little toy on the floor, *But that is getting old*, he thought. He looked towards his window and decided to continue with his second favorite hobby: spying on the people of his *contrada* to make sure they were all doing what was right. The neighbor girl was on his list of people to be watched.

Ever since he had caused himself to bump into the girl, Olivetti felt that the girl was up to something that wasn't proper for a good Sienese girl. Looking out of his window, he had seen her go out by herself another time in the morning and then return home alone when the sun was about to set. She carried no meats or vegetables with her. So, she wasn't going to the market.

If she wasn't going to the market but was going out by herself in the morning, what could she be up to? I will look for a pattern. When she leaves in the morning, I will put my militia spy skills into action. This could be interesting.

And so on the next morning Olivetti woke up when the rooster crowed. He put on clothing other than his usual *contrada* uniform and pulled his cap over his forehead. He stared out his window.

When Olivetti saw the girl leave her house, he scurried down the stairs to follow her at a safe distance. Painfully but successfully, Olivetti managed to follow her for about eight blocks until she entered the large piazza by the Palazzo Pubblico. He made certain to see what street she would enter after leaving the piazza. *Buona fortuna!* He said to himself. *I see that she is exiting at the Via della Città. Tomorrow I will hatch part two of my plan.*

And so on the next morning, the corporal woke up even earlier than he had the day before and dragged his old legs as quickly as he could to the piazza. He stood by a merchant's stall at the entrance to the *Via della Città*. In a short while, he spotted Elisabetta coming across the piazza towards the *via*. Olivetti turned to the side so that the girl would not recognize him. Once she began traversing down the *Via dellal Città* Olivetti integrated into the crowd of people going to work and followed her as she turned onto the *Via di Stalloreggi*.

After passing about eight buildings, the girl entered a three- story building that was wider than it was tall. Olivetti pretended he was looking inside the door of a goldsmith's shop across the street and down a short distance. He turned his head slightly to watch as the girl pushed open a large, heavy door at the entrance of the building.

Within about five minutes after the girl entered the building, a young man came out and opened the door widely---keeping it open with a wooden wedge. Smiling and whistling a tune, the young man went back into the building, came out with a long pole, and then used it to open the shutters. The young man proceeded to bring out a couple of long shelves upon which he placed pieces of art and decorated objects. Once he arranged everything to his liking, the individual stood next to the shelves and tried to get the attention of passersby so they might stop and purchase the wares.

To see what the girl was doing inside the building, the corporal decided to pretend to be a potential customer. Nonchalantly, he hobbled over to where the young man was and inquired as to whether he was selling the objects.

Pointing to the shelves, the young man replied, "Oh yes, good sir, you can see that we have small paintings of the Blessed Mother, carved wooden crosses and blank books with beautiful hand-painted covers."

"*Meraviglioso!*" Olivetti exclaimed. "Are there more of these beautiful objects for sale inside?"

"*Si, si Signore,*" the apprentice said as he ushered the corporal into a small corner in the front of the workshop where goods were sold. "*Per favore, scusi, Signore,* I must help a customer outside now. But feel free to see if anything catches your fancy here."

"*Grazie,*" the corporal said with the best smile he could summon. Olivetti pulled his cap over his forehead and looked to see where the girl might be. When Olivetti looked to his right, he saw several people gathered around an immense piece of wood. Each was performing a different task, and there in the midst of them was the very man whom he wholeheartedly despised, Duccio di Buoninsegna.

Olivetti immediately put down his head so that Duccio would not see him. However, he soon observed that Duccio was so absorbed in talking to one of his apprentices that he would not notice him. The apprentice was sitting on the floor and was appearing to grind and mix a couple of substances together with what Olivetti thought was a mortar and pestle.

Olivetti's eyes popped wide open as he noticed that the apprentice was someone he recognized. She did not speak; she only listened and nodded. With her gray hood drawn slightly over her brow, she looked more like a "he" than a "she." However, that familiar gray hood and faded orange smock told Olivetti that it was the neighbor girl.

Quickly Olivetti turned and walked out of the building.

Out of the corner of his eye, Duccio saw a shadow leaving the premises and called, "Mimmo, was there a customer inside who needed help?"

"*Si,* Master Duccio, but he left so quickly that I could not be of service to him."

So now Corporal Olivetti concluded that he could get two people in trouble for breaking Siena's rules: the neighbor girl for working as an apprentice and Duccio for having her as an apprentice… and perhaps as more than an apprentice. The corporal laughed in a high, shrill voice that sounded more like a cackle.

Ah, my treasured window, Olivetti thought. *Everyday I shall sit by it as the sun begins to set and watch for the neighbor girl to come home alone.*

On the very next afternoon, as the shadows were lengthening, he saw the girl walking hastily from the direction of the piazza. And she was alone.

Olivetti rose quickly from his sitting position and ran down the stairs so rapidly that he almost tripped. However, he would sacrifice anything if he could position himself to bump into the girl right in front of his tower. His efforts were successful.

The old man rushed outside and deliberately slammed into the girl. "Where have you been young lady at this time of day…and by…yourself?"

Elisabetta would not allow herself to be intimidated by the corporal this time. "What right do you have to ask me where I have been or where I am going?"

"I am the COR-POR-AL," Olivetti said as he emphasized each syllable of his rank. "And as such, young lady, I have been granted the public's trust in this *contrada* to make sure everyone is…is…behaving as they should."

"*Scusi*, let me by, I have to go home," Elisabetta said as she rushed away before he could utter another word.

Even though he couldn't get the girl to admit where she had been, Olivetti believed he was heaping up evidence for a final blow to Duccio's reputation. He could taste victory. It was sweet, but there was an aftertaste of bitterness that Olivetti found puzzling.

PART THREE

JUNE 19-26, 1311

CHAPTER 12

JUNE 19, 1311

Taviana arose at dawn, dressed, and told her half-asleep husband that she was going to the Cathedral for morning mass. This was no surprise to Duccio who admired his wife for her faithfulness to the Good Lord.

As Taviana passed by him, Duccio pulled himself up from their bed, put an arm around his wife, gave her an easy hug, and told her to remember him in her prayers. Even though there was a bit of glory connected to being his wife since the installation, Duccio knew that Taviana had put up with a lot from him, and he appreciated that she stuck with him through good times and bad.

After returning Duccio's hug, Taviana walked down to the first floor and left their home/workshop before the apprentices arrived. The many people who knew Taviana greeted her from their doorsteps or from the streets, and she returned their salutations.

Upon arriving at the cathedral, Taviana went to a confessional booth. It was her habit to go to confession on a regular basis to lay out her sins to whoever happened to be the priest on duty, but she always preferred confessing to Father Giacobi. Although a panel with little holes was supposed to hide the identity of the priest and the confessor, Taviana could always tell when she was speaking with Father Giacobi, because she heard his voice frequently at morning mass.

In fact, what Taviana liked best about this priest was his voice: calm, quiet, and exuding acceptance of her when she was in the confessional booth--- regardless of how she thought she had sinned.

Her sins usually revolved around her feeling disrespectful towards her husband. On one occasion, she confessed, "I threw a cup at my husband after he was out almost all night." Another time she bowed her head and said, "*Mio sposo* received another summons to appear in court for an unpaid debt. I told him that I wish I would have never married him."

On both occasions, Father Giacobi, had told her, "God forgives you. And He will reward you rather than punish you for your untold patience with your husband."

One time when Taviana was telling a story of how she reacted to Duccio when he came home late smelling like a cask of wine, the priest gently asked her, "Do you think *Signor* Duccio was doing anything to…to… violate your marriage vows? I must tell you that God forgives a woman from separating from a man if he is unfaithful."

Taviana jumped a little from her confessional seat, "No, no good Father, I know that my husband loves me and me alone. The day after his carousing he is always regretful and tells me how much he appreciates me…even if I don't want to hear it at the time. And almost always he is good to me with all of the little things of life."

She had continued, "What makes him *pazzo* at times is his art. His mind gives him no rest when he is planning his pictures and then deciding how to paint them. And then he has to make sure he gets paid so that he can give *soldi* to his apprentices and buy materials. He has explained to me that he needs to "let loose", as he calls it, once in awhile and that's…that's why he goes to the *taverna*."

However, on this particular day in the booth, Taviana was feeling content with her husband and actually had to look for sins to confess. She greeted whomever was behind the confessional screen by saying, "Hello, Father."

Much to her pleasure, it was Father Giacobi's voice that replied, "Hello Child of God."

When Taviana heard his greeting, she smiled and looked forward to this confession.

Taviana replied, "I am so happy today that it is hard for me to find anything to trouble my soul…With my husband's Maestà being so joyously received and my dear Duccio feeling less *stressato*, I have had no problems lately."

Father Giacobi was quiet. Taviana wondered what the hesitation was. Usually her favorite priest had taken an attitude of reassurance and kindness when she spoke. Now that she was happy he didn't seem very happy for her.

She finally broke the silence. "Is there something wrong, Father?"

While considering that he shouldn't let his personal opinions get in the way, Father Giacobi asked anyway, "Dear Child, this is a little difficult for me to ask, but don't you think that your husband's altarpiece is just a little too… may I say…worldly?"

"Oh, but Father why would you say that?"

"Well, the front of the altarpiece that you and the worshippers see is not too bad…"

"Oh, Father with all due respect, I love looking at the front of the altarpiece with the Blessed Virgin looking so lovingly at her Son… the faces of those sweet angels making me feel like God really does send them to…"

The priest interrupted, "Truthfully…It's the back of the altarpiece that bothers me most. I know your husband worked very hard on creating this artwork and that you are happy that the Maestà has been well-received by our fair citizens, but have you noticed how your husband depicted Christ on all of the scenes on the back of the altarpiece?"

"Well, Father, when *mio sposo* paints, I do not watch what he is doing but when I got a quick look at the back, the pictures seemed fine to me. What was not to your liking, Father?"

How can I say this without offending this devout woman? Giacobi thought.

After a short pause, he said, "Fortunately, the worshippers will only be exposed to the front of the Maestà for the most part, although they are free to look at the back if it is an overflow service or they just look around the cathedral." The priest paused and then said, "I will try to explain as respectfully as I can what I object to on the back. I am thinking…I am thinking… about the scene where Christ is supposedly entering Jerusalem where he will be crucified in a short time…"

"Yes, Father, I remember that scene."

The priest continued, "Although He is seated on a donkey, the Good Lord looks holy enough with His beautiful golden halo and His azure blue cloak. Your husband did a good job there. But when he depicts all of the people in Jerusalem being the same size as Jesus, I object. A while back I went to Santa Maria Novella Church in Florence for the induction of a new priest. On this trip, I was fortunate enough to see your husband's depiction of Jesus and the Virgin and the Franciscan monks. Did you happen to see that painting before *Signor* Duccio delivered it to Florence?"

"Oh, yes, Father, I did think that was a precious painting, and I recall how Mary and Jesus were gigantic in comparison to the three little friars worshipping at the hem of Mary's gown."

"See, my Child, that's what I mean. It has been our solemn tradition to elevate Mary and Jesus above us mere men…and women…to make them much bigger than us…in our art."

Taviana fell silent.

"Another point I would like to make, dear child, is that your husband probably meant well, but it was somewhat sacrilegious that in scenes such as that of Christ Entering Jerusalem he used the faces of real citizens of Siena like… Fabrizio the barber …and even Giovanni the rag seller to be, of all people, Peter…." Taviana could hear the priest take a deep breath before he said, "I can't help but feel that this diminishes the holiness of the altarpiece."

By now Taviana was asking herself, *Why is Father Giacobi telling me all this? It is ruining the joy I was feeling when I entered the Cathedral.*

Giacobi realized that he had probably overstepped the boundaries between priest and penitent by divulging his true feelings in this manner. *What got a hold of me?* He questioned himself.

Trying to conclude this confessional on a more familiar note, Father Giacobi said, "Dear Child of God, we may not agree on this subject, but you came here to confess your sins today. What sins do you have to confess?"

Taviana thought for a while and then offered, "I confess, Father, that on three occasions in the last week I yelled loudly at my grandchildren who live with us and that I denied giving alms to a beggar when I had five *denari* in my pocket."

"Then if you are truly penitent, dear Child of God, go in peace. Your sins are forgiven."

And that was that. Taviana walked down the cathedral steps feeling unsettled. But within a short while, she pulled herself together and used her walk home to plan what she would cook that day for lunch.

CHAPTER 13

JUNE 20, 1311

Dripping from contentment just eleven days after the parade and not yet busy with a new commission, Duccio decided to use his precious free time to take his favorite journey and visit his vineyard. It was the mark of a successful Sienese man to own a vineyard. And so when Duccio received his commission money from his small Maestà nine years earlier, he bought his property to stake his claim to fame. The wine from the grapes kept his casks full at home and the sale of the remainder actually brought in a small profit.

Desiring some companionship for his trip, Duccio had asked Taviana to go with him. However, she declined saying her knee bothered her and she did not feel she had the strength for the journey. Duccio was a little *nervoso* about going alone, because it was not a full two weeks since his finger pricking had warned him that evil could come soon. But Duccio's uncle had always reassured him that if he heeded an omen by being very careful and doing all he could to prevent danger, he could rest in the comfort that after about two weeks he would be safe. There were only three days left, and he was being very cautious about everything.

So, Duccio set forth on his trip alone. On a warm, sunny afternoon without a cloud in the sky, Duccio donned his leg coverings, a comfortable tunic, and a cloak with a hood. Taviana fixed him some food, and he put it in a cloth bundle that he tied on a stick over his shoulder. And, of course, he brought his favorite walking stick.

To depart from Siena, Duccio walked about eight blocks from his home, through the neighboring *contrada*, and then towards the *Porta San Marco*. When he reached the gate, the keepers shouted a cheerful *Buon Viaggio* to the painter whom they recognized from the parade with the Maestà. However, no matter who the person was, the gatekeepers were less concerned about who was departing than about who was entering the fortified walls of Siena.

As soon as Duccio walked through the gate, he was smitten by the sight of the verdant hills of his beloved Tuscan countryside. He loved the way the rolling hills took on a variegated geometric pattern. There were squares of olive gardens, vineyards, and horse farms---each having different lines, textures, and shades of green and brown. To Duccio, it was The Garden of Eden. Sometimes he yearned to move to the country with Taviana, but as long as he needed the *soldi* and loved creating, he would have to put up with the sounds and smells of industry in Siena.

Duccio braced his legs as usual as he went down the rather steep hill on which Siena was located. After he made the descent, he followed a dirt path pounded down through the centuries by people going to and from the city. Usually it took him about half of an afternoon to walk to his vineyard, but seeing as how he was aging, Duccio thought it

The Vineyard

might take longer. He didn't account, though, for the energy he experienced coming off of the successful parade with the Maestà.

With time alone and away from the fray of everyday life, Duccio's mind returned to his longing for Peace of Mind. That's all he ever had desired. He just wanted to do his art and not be bothered by anything else---except his beloved family. But Tension and Obsession had been his all too frequent companions.

Now that I am becoming an old man, I will continue to create great art. But I will steer away from controversy. I'll do what my patrons want with few questions asked. I will not allow myself to become obsessed with constantly figuring out new ideas for my art. I will accrue a small fortune. I will attend mass at times to view my Maestà. And when the good Lord comes to carry me away and I leave my blessed Taviana for a while, I will join my parents and they will finally be proud of me as we look down upon the Maestà together.

In the midst of his dreams for the future, Duccio found himself arriving at the entrance of his vineyard. He looked at the location of the sun, and it told him that he had covered the territory at just a little slower pace than last time. Duccio smiled.

Nine years ago, he and his vintner had fashioned a simple gate of tree limbs with one limb going across the top and bearing the sign, "The Vineyard of Duccio di Buoninsegna." Soon after passing through the gate, Duccio was greeted by two little children---one of whom took his hand and said, *"Buon giorno, Signore,* come and see *la mia famiglia."* The children hopped so quickly to the family home that Duccio could hardly keep up with them.

As they approached the doorway of the house, the children yelled, "Grandfather, Grandmother, *Papà,* someone has come to see us."

Duccio lowered his head to keep from hitting the beam over the doorway. He spotted a seated young man who smiled at him but did not rise to greet him. Duccio had been afraid that Luca and Rosa---the manager and his wife---might be taking their afternoon nap. Actually, the children did awaken them from their last moments of rest, but the two of them came from their bed behind a hanging piece of cloth and greeted Duccio with laughter.

Luca slowly walked towards Duccio, gave him a firm handshake and said, *"Signor* Duccio, it is so nice to see you!" Duccio noticed that Luca had changed somewhat since he had last visited the vineyard six months ago: he was slightly hunched over and had some difficulty walking. But he had not lost his magnanimous personality. He said, "*Signor* Duccio, the grapes are *fantastiche* this summer---they will be our plumpest and juiciest ever!"

Duccio walked over to Rosa who was crying somewhat and smiling at the same time. He gave her a little hug as she said, "Welcome, *Signor* Duccio, we have missed you."

Then Duccio sat on a chair that the young man gestured for him to take. Everything was just as Duccio remembered it---the simple little painting of the Virgin setting on the ledge of their fireplace, the old wooden table covered with cuts and grooves, the four large chairs and two small ones, the muslin screen hanging from the rafters to divide the living areas.

As the children sat on the little chairs, Luca gestured towards the young man in the corner, "You remember our son Sandro here? He fell off a ladder last week and hurt his back, but he should be healed soon..."

"*Signor* Duccio, it is so nice to see you again," Sandro said. "My wife is doing my work in the vineyard today along with my brother Galgano, but she will be happy to see you also. How was your journey?"

"To tell you the truth, my journey seemed easy even though I am becoming an old man. The time seemed to fly by. How are you folks? And, *per favore*, tell me more about how the vineyard is doing."

Luca gave Duccio a summary of the activity in the vineyard and offered him a glass of wine from a newly opened cask.

"*Buonissimo*!" Duccio exclaimed. "You are as good a wine maker as ever! And I am *contento* to hear your report that the grapes are healthy this year which will make for more *eccellente vino*."

After Luca and Duccio discussed the income received from merchants buying their wine, Duccio asked Rosa to give him a report on how each of their children was doing. Rosa told him a little about each and then mentioned how proud she was of her son in Siena who was a priest.

"Since I do so much work with the churches in Siena, I know many of the priests," Duccio said. "What is the name of your son?"

"The son of whom I am speaking is Father Giacobi. He is a priest at the Siena Cathedral."

Duccio almost fell off of his chair. He had no idea that Father Giacobi was the son of his vintner. How different the very formal Father Giacobi was from his warm, loving parents who were serving him wine and talking with him in such a relaxed manner.

Luca noticed Duccio's reaction to this information. "Do you know our son?"

"Well…yes…I know your son. I don't know if you are aware of the large Maestà altarpiece that I just completed for the Siena Cathedral…"

Rosa interrupted, "*Scusi,* one of my other sons who lives in Siena told me that he had a day off for the parade, but I didn't now it was you who created the Maestà!"

Luca got up and shook Duccio's hand with the strength of a twenty year old. "*Congratulazione*!" We know that you are a great artist, but this…this…"

"*Grazie, grazie.* The people of Siena seemed to love the altarpiece when we brought it from my workshop to the Cathedral just a couple of weeks ago, and the bishop spoke highly of it…but…to tell you the truth, my friends, your son did not seem to approve of it."

"Oh, I am so sorry," winced Rosa.

Luca said, "That boy was always so *prudente*…the smartest of all our children…but so particular about doing things in just a certain way…"

"*Sì*," Sandro chimed in. "When we were little and picking grapes, Giacobi would try to get me to do it just so. He would tell me that I couldn't just tear the grapes off of the vine. I should slowly and gently release them from their stems like so," he said as he raised one hand, put his fingers together and slowly pulled down an invisible grape. "If I ate a grape or two, he would scold me. One day he watched me for a whole hour as he picked grapes next to me. He tried to be a gentle teacher, but he corrected me every time I pulled on a grape or ate one."

Sandro gently pinched the toes of his little girl who was sitting on his lap and said to her, "I still eat a grape or two when we are picking in the vineyard, don't I, *mia bambina?*"

The girl smiled back at her father and laughed at their little crime.

Rosa shook her head and said, "Yes, that was our Giacobi…If I may be so bold to ask…What does he not like about your Maestà?"

"I will tell you what I think he objects to, but please do not take this as a criticism of your son. He is a very devoted priest…"

"Continue, please," Rosa said.

"I think he objected to my putting a prayer on Mary's throne and signing my name to it. We artists have never put our name on a piece of holy work…"

"A small thing," Luca said, "But was there anything else?"

"Your son and I were on the planning committee for the Maestà, and he didn't like me making Jesus the same size as the common people and mingling with them on an equal level."

"That sounds like Giacobi," responded Luca. "To him, the Blessed Mother and Jesus must always be gigantic and regal---nothing like real people. He never cared much for our little humble country church with its simple crucifixes and small paintings of the holy family."

Rosa said, "I would like to talk with Giacobi about his being so…so… critical of your altarpiece, but it is so hard to see him…they only let the priests see their families once every eight months."

"Ah, don't you worry, Rosa. Everything will be fine," Duccio said.

"But I do worry, *Signor* Duccio. Once when we were able to visit Giacobi I reminded him that I hope he is learning to accept people---even himself--- even if they weren't his idea of perfect. I remember him saying something like: "*Mamma,* as a priest I hear confessions by people that run shivers through my spine. But I know that God loves them and forgives them if they are truly sorry."

"Then I asked him something else. If people just do things differently than you, can you accept that also?"

Luca asked, "And what did our son say?"

"*Certamente, Mamma,* he said, but his voice sounded well ...well...weak ... like he wasn't so certain."

Then Duccio changed the subject. Until the last ember of the fire died out, he and the family chatted idly about more pleasant things and eventually drifted off to sleep.

In the morning, Duccio woke up and set forth for home. His legs were slightly sluggish due to the plentiful wine that he drank the night before. However, he sang almost all of the way home. The only time he stopped singing was when he thought about how he had to tackle one very unpleasant task when he returned home.

CHAPTER 14

JUNE 22, 1311

Duccio waited until the workday was almost over, and then he called Elisabetta into his office.

The artist pulled out a chair for his apprentice and looked towards her with a gaze that was unusual for him. The lids on his eyes drooped, and they averted direct contact with those of Elisabetta.

Speaking slowly, Duccio began his pre-planned speech: "Well, we did it Elisabetta. Just over a week ago we got the Maestà installed, and people loved it. We certainly worked hard on that altarpiece, but if it didn't touch the people, all of our labor would have been in vain."

"How can I ever express my appreciation for the great job you did--- especially with mixing my colors so perfectly and doing the gilding so precisely? Introducing your father to me was a Godsend, too. And thanks for posing for my angels. The people loved them."

Elisabetta was not accustomed to Duccio speaking to her like this. "You are saying all these nice things, *Signor* Duccio, but, if I may be so bold to ask… do you have something else on your mind?"

"My faithful apprentice, Elisabetta, I might as well get to the point. It pains me to tell you this, but I think it is time for your apprenticeship to end and for you to get on with your life."

Immediately Elisabetta slumped in her chair. Duccio swallowed hard and continued, "Sooner or later---and probably sooner---someone is going to figure out that you are a female working in this shop. Then…it will be bad… Probably both you and I will be…tormented and shunned."

Unwelcome sobs and tears came pouring out of Elisabetta. She put her hands to her face and tried to wipe away the wetness.

Duccio continued, "People would never understand 'the gift,' how you have it, and why I let you…well…open it here."

"But where will I go and what will I do? I need to paint." Elisabetta pulled at her tunic as if to rid herself of this problem. "I knew the time would come when I would have to leave. I saw you let go of Ambrogio and Simone. And I prayed that somehow my day would not come."

Silently Duccio pondered for a little while about how he could soften the blow and offer Elisabetta a morsel of hope.

Finally he said, "Remain in the workshop for another two weeks. Every afternoon when you are ready to go home I will give you a small quantity of material for colors to take with you…even a little lapus lazuli and gold."

He thought some more. "I will also send home with you some gesso and a few brushes---all of which you will have to hide under your tunic."

"*Molte grazie, Signor* Duccio," Elisabetta said quietly between soft sobs. "But what will I do when I run out?"

"I know it may be difficult for you, but you will probably have to take on the Sienese womanly jobs of cooking, cleaning, embroidering…going to the market."

"Not just that…I need more!" responded Elisabetta.

Then Duccio stood up and said, "Your parents have been very understanding of you and have allowed you to do something very daring by being my *clandestino* apprentice for a long time. But now things have to change."

"I know, I know."

"Perhaps your parents can come up with a dowry and arrange a marriage for you that will bless you as much as Taviana and I have been blessed."

Elisabetta forced a smile and stood up. "*Grazie* for everything *Signor* Duccio. I will appreciate the art supplies. I don't think I will ever again be as happy as I have been at your workshop."

"It's not like you're going to the gallows," Duccio smiled.

As Elisabetta slowly plodded to the door, Duccio said, "*Arrivederci* until tomorrow, Paolo."

Because Mimmo had just approached Duccio's door to hear what was going on, Elisabetta almost bumped into him as she made her exit.

"*Scusi*," fumbled Mimmo. "I was just…just walking to the work table to deposit some brushes."

When he saw Elisabetta's countenance, he asked, "What is wrong, Paolo? I'm sorry you can't talk but…"

"Can't talk? Well, I can talk. Do you hear my voice?" Elisabetta said loudly.

"What? What? I most certainly do hear your voice, but what happened? If you got your voice, you don't seem…very happy…"

"All right, Mimmo, you might as well know that I am a girl and I can talk."

Mimmo swayed slightly and held onto the edge of the work table near him.

"*Signor* Duccio had to get rid of me. I will be back tomorrow but then only for a couple of weeks."

Mimmo regained his senses somewhat and saw that the sun was setting as Elisabetta opened the door to go outside. He said, "Let…let…me walk you home. A young," he hesitated for a moment and then continued, "woman should not walk without a chaperone at night or even at dusk."

"Oh, all right," said Elisabetta.

"And by the way, what is your real name…since you are a girl?"

"Elisabetta," she replied. And so began the new life of the former apprentice previously known as Paolo.

Once Mimmo safely deposited Elisabetta at her doorstep, he had the opportunity to think about what all of this news meant. And it brought a smile to his face.

CHAPTER 15

JUNE 23, 1311

Since it was nearly three weeks since the Maestà had been paraded to the Cathedral, Corporal Olivetti reasoned that the excitement about the panel had subsided. After gaining the approval of Father Giacobi, Olivetti woke up early and made his way from his home to the Palazzo Pubblico.

When he passed through the Palazzo's marble portico, he went straight to the complaint department.

Olivetti hobbled up to the tall counter of the secretary and used his strongest voice to ask, "*Per favore*, could I speak with one of the Council of Nine today?"

Recognizing his regular guest, the clerk said quietly, "I will see if I can find one of the Nine for you, Corporal Olivetti. I believe that *Signor* Rocco Lippi may be available to consider what is …probably a complaint from you today?"

"*Si*, it is most certainly a complaint."

When the clerk informed Lippi that Olivetti was in the waiting room, Lippi frowned. The clerk smiled slightly and shrugged his shoulders.

However, *Signor* Lippi dutifully rose from his chair to usher Olivetti into his office.

"Greetings, Corporal, what might be bringing you to the Palazzo on this fine summer day?"

After a hasty "*Buon giorno*," Olivetti slowly walked into Lippi's office.

Lippi motioned Olivetti to sit in front of a large oak desk that smelled like a freshly cut tree. The chairs were newly stained with a coating that made Olivetti crinkle his nose for a moment.

Olivetti began, "It is a pleasure to sit with you in your fine new office today, *Signor* Lippi, but my reason for coming is not a pleasant one. The violation that I must inform you about today is probably more serious than any other that I have had to bring into court... It involves a very famous man who has done a very bad thing."

"Let me guess. Could this be about Duccio di Buoninsegna?"

When Olivetti said, "Yes," Lippi tipped back his chair slightly and let Olivetti unfurl his story. Olivetti detailed how he had seen Elisabetta walk home on two occasions by herself as the sun was setting and how he had followed her to Duccio's workshop and saw that she was working for him.

"In conclusion," the corporal said, "Duccio is once again flaunting society's rules. As always, he thinks he is above the law. Having a female apprentice and allowing a girl to leave his workshop unescorted at night...well it's a violation of all of the rules of proper behavior that we Sienese hold so dear!"

Devoid of facial expression, Lippi sat quietly for a minute or so and then said, "I do not regard this as a serious matter."

The corporal sputtered, "What, what?"

"Yes, the behaviors you mention are against the way we Sienese usually do things, but I do not know if there is a law on the books that states a woman cannot be an apprentice. I believe that some widows work as apprentices..."

"But the girl coming home at night by herself?" Olivetti pleaded.

Rising from his chair, Lippi said, "I can see why you disapprove. Perhaps you could talk to the girl's parents about her being unescorted, but aside from that, I don't think you have a legal leg to stand on."

Olivetti took his time pulling himself out of the chair. Without a mere nod of farewell, he walked out of the office and then into the light of day.

After mumbling to himself, kicking a few loose stones on the *via*, and shaking his cane at a boy chasing an errant ball, Corporal Olivetti regained his composure. *I will have to return to the Council of Nine with a description of Duccio's behavior that is just too outrageous to ignore!*

CHAPTER 16

JUNE 26, 1311

Olivetti had paid Father Giacobi a visit the day after talking with *Signor* Lippi. Father Giacobi listened to his story about how Lippi had dismissed Olivetti's complaints against Duccio and his female apprentice.

"If only Lippi had agreed to hear my case," Olivetti had lamented. "Everything would have been perfect. Duccio's morals would have been questioned in a court of law, we could have told the Bishop about this and you could have made your case about the back of the Maestà being too worldly."

"And you would have gotten some more revenge for Duccio not doing his military duties…" the priest said quietly as he frowned with his disapproval of the revenge factor.

But then Olivetti told Giacobi of his alternative plan---one that could lead to much more dramatic consequences.

Now Father Giacobi was fighting a battle within himself---a battle between means and ends. He felt that "the end" of hiding the sacrilegious part of Duccio's painting was a worthy one. But he wasn't sure if Olivetti's "means" to this end was a justifiable one.

"Oh *Dio* mio," sighed the priest as he lay on his bed that night.

Father Giacobi didn't think that Duccio would have committed the sin that Olivetti implied. Furthermore, he knew that to bring this into court would break the sweet heart of poor Taviana. He felt he had to think long and hard about Olivetti's proposal and maybe even do a little praying about it. After all, he was a priest. But for some reason Father Giacobi didn't feel right discussing this with God.

To the extent that the priest worried that Olivetti's move was the wrong one the corporal was sure it was the right one. Unbeknownst to Father Giacobi, Olivetti decided on the way home from talking with the priest that he would collect evidence to bring his plan to fruition.

PART FOUR

JULY 18-26, 1311

CHAPTER 17

JULY, 18, 1311

After she had to leave her apprenticeship with Duccio, Elisabetta suffered through a broken heart from which she thought she would never heal. Her recuperation came from her art. Her parents saw how bereft Betta was, and they went to any lengths they realistically could to make her happy again. She asked her father for whatever small pieces of wood he could bring home so that she could coat them with gesso and paint on them.

Now that she did not have to work for a master, Elisabetta could create whatever she wanted with the little supply of paints from Duccio. At first, it was difficult for her to know what she wanted to paint. Then she decided to capture whatever she saw around her---without having any message to her work. She painted a bowl of fruit, a wooden table with a lace tablecloth and a candle on it, and the front door with its grainy surface. Her parents and brother were amazed that she imbued these simple objects with beauty and dignity.

Then Elisabetta asker her family members to sit for her while she sketched them. They said they couldn't spare much time from their chores, but she succeeded in getting each one to hold still for short periods. Then she began painting their portraits from the sketches she had made. Until she was done with each painting, she would stare at the family member model for as much time as she could to catch each one's eye color, skin shade and expression.

Her brother said to her one day, "I don't like to be stared at all the time, Betta."

Betta stuck out her tongue at him, and they both laughed.

After that, a sense of relaxation returned to the household. Her family was amazed at the portraits and pictures of simple objects that Elisabetta was producing. However, they were also somewhat frightened. They were fearful, because women were not supposed to paint and because her pictures were not of the usual religious scenes.

What would happen if someone found out about our little family secret? Anna asked herself.

One day Elisabetta had an unexpected visitor. Upon hearing the knock on the door, her mother went to see who it was. It was Mimmo from Duccio's workshop.

"*Buon giorno,*" Mimmo said to Elisabetta's mother. "I have come to inquire about your good daughter's health."

Anna did not say anything, but she turned and looked towards Elisabetta who was smiling widely.

"All right, you may come in, but just for a short while."

When Elisabetta saw Mimmo, she felt like hugging him but simply said, "Mimmo, it is so nice to see you again. Come in and tell me about how things are going at the shop."

"First, how are you Paolo…ah…Elisabetta?"

"I am all right now. It's been so hard to be away from you and Master Duccio and all of the activity of the workshop, but I am surviving. Tell me… if you don't mind…what has been going on?"

"Well, *Signor* Duccio has received a new commission for a small Maestà for a church at the city of Massa Marittima. Do you know where that is?"

"I think Father had to build something there. It was about a three day's journey by foot and near the sea…if I remember right."

Mimmo nodded in agreement.

Leaning forward, Elisabetta asked, "What…what are *Signor* Duccio's ideas for this new Maestà?"

"A priest and someone else came to talk with him. When they left, Duccio muttered that he would do what they said without trying to put in his own way of doing things too much."

"Do you know what they asked of him to do?"

"He said something about how they wanted him to work most on the Crucifixion Scene."

Elisabetta smiled, "I bet he is so deep in thought that the workshop could set on fire…God forbid…and he wouldn't even notice."

"You have that correct. *Signore* sits at his desk and draws, then gets up and paces, then sits down and stares, then draws some more. Since I am the only one working in the shop now, I must admit that it makes me a little…a little… *nervoso*, but I respect *Signor* Duccio so much that I never would complain."

At that moment, Anna announced from the corner where she was cooking, "Dinner will be served soon. Your friend must be going, Betta."

"*Si, si, Signora* and *grazie* for the time you allowed me to speak with your daughter," Mimmo said, and when he looked over to where Anna was, he noticed some small paintings leaning against the wall. He tried to get a closer look at them, but Anna shooed him out the door before he could do so.

After Mimmo left, Elisabetta found herself in such a state of reverie that she could hardly respond when any of her family members said anything. However, she looked *contenta,* and that was enough for the family.

CHAPTER 18

JULY 19, 1311

The next morning when Mimmo returned to work he could hardly wait to tell Duccio about his visit with Elisabetta. Duccio immediately inquired as to how she was doing and what her demeanor was.

"She seemed lonely but not completely…hopeless," Mimmo said.

"Oh, good. I have been so worried about her…"

"Her mother couldn't wait to get rid of me, though."

"You know how our Sienese mothers are."

"I know, but I could hardly keep from looking at Elisabetta's beautiful brown eyes…"

"Mimmo!"

"I just can't believe that she's a girl…a woman…I still feel like calling her Paolo. And here I thought there was something a little…different…about me, because I cared for her so much when she was working here. But anyhow,

I wanted to say also that I noticed she had done some paintings… they were lying against the wall."

Now Duccio increased the intensity of his blue-eyed gaze at Mimmo. "And what did they look like, Mimmo?"

"They were unlike most paintings that I see in Siena. They were of flowers… and doors…and faces…"

"Did they look good to you?"

"Si, *Signor* Duccio, you know that I have never been one to be able to explain art, but to me, they were cheerful and…very real looking. Now that I think about it, there was one that looked just like her brother Tommaso."

Silence filled the room. Then Duccio said, "I have an idea, Mimmo. I think I will make a *cassone* (chest) for Elisabetta. One like the kind the city government had me make for their records. Now families who have the *soldi* are commissioning artists to paint *cassoni* for their daughters. Some even call them "hope chests.""

"And why do they call this type of *cassone*…"a hope chest"?"

"For the simple reason that a girl can put into the chest items like linens, plates, candlesticks, and whatever other household items she can accumulate in hopes of getting a good husband someday."

"I guess Elisabetta would like that," Mimmo mused.

Thinking aloud, Duccio said, "The most important part of the chest for Elisabetta, though, would be that she could store her paintings in it until she felt the time was right---if ever---for her to show them to the world. If that time never comes, at least she could enjoy looking at them herself."

More silence occurred until Duccio came up with another idea. "Mimmo, would you be kind enough to return to Elisabetta's home within the next couple of days and inquire of Elisabetta's parents as to whether they would allow me to make this *cassone* and try to explain to them the reasons why I want to make the *cassone*?"

"Si, the *cassone* would be a…a…"hope chest" for her and would also have room for her paintings. Correct, *Signor* Duccio?"

"That is correct. And one more thing. Could you inquire with Elisabetta's father as to whether he could supply me with the poplar I need for the chest?"

"I will do my best to explain all of this *Signor* Duccio. I must admit that the thought of seeing Elisabetta again will make me work my very hardest to get all of this right."

Then Duccio said, "Back to work. I have a painting to get done," and Duccio moved around with the fervor Mimmo was used to see him exerting. As Duccio got out his charcoal to do his sketching, he said to himself, *Life feels good. Hearing that Elisabetta is surviving is a relief. I have a new commission. And it's been over a month since I pricked my finger. Perhaps Peace of Mind and Buona Fortuna will finally remain with me for a while.*

CHAPTER 19

JULY 21, 1311

Olivetti woke up with a mission. He was ready to obtain the "proof" for his charge.

As everyone was rushing to work, Olivetti headed to the Piazza del Campo where he rested for fifteen minutes and bought a small loaf from one of the bakers. Freshly baked bread was a treat of aroma and taste that Olivetti seldom allowed himself. Day old bread was cheaper.

"Ah," Olivetti sighed as he took a bite of bread and commenced on his journey. The rest of the walk to Duccio's workshop was not far but it did create a challenge, because on this side of the *via* most of the walkers were going towards the piazza, and Olivetti was going against the stream. When he took a second large bite of his bread, a man unwittingly brushed against him and knocked the loaf out of his hand.

"*Terribile!*" Olivetti said trying to scold the speedily departing offender.

When he finally arrived in the vicinity of Duccio's workshop, Olivetti smiled. *And now here comes my golden opportunity.*

Olivetti decided to stand across the street and a couple of houses down from Duccio's workshop, and then he surveyed the people going to and fro. They looked like they were quite intent on whatever each wanted to accomplish. Finally he noticed a young man standing a couple of doors down on the same side of the street as he was. The man was in no apparent rush to go anywhere. Olivetti hobbled over to speak with him.

The corporal tipped his cap to him and began, "Good sir, I would greatly appreciate it if I could let you know about a serious matter that has arisen recently in this *contrada*. I am a corporal from the San Donato *Contrada*…"

The man held his hand out to shake Olivetti's. "Pleased to meet you *Signore*. I am Bartolomeo…"

"Well, we who have the responsibilities of being a corporal have been told to spread the word in this *contrada* about a serious problem here…"

"Oh, no, what is the problem, Corporal?"

"I have been told that there has been some thievery recently in this *contrada* and that people should be on the lookout for this."

"That is quite alarming, *Signore*," the young man said with eyes opening widely. "Can you tell me about the details?"

"No one knows who the robbers are, but the residents say that the robbers have broken into two different towers while the owners are gone."

"*Dio mio!* I have two small *bambini*. My wife and I will certainly have to bolt the doors at all times now."

Having caught the interest of the young man, Olivetti decided to get to his real point. "I have heard that there is a workshop on this street owned by Duccio di Buoninsegna."

"*Sì*, we are rather proud that Duccio is our neighbor…seeing as how he is the artist who created the beautiful Maestà."

"Ah, but I regret to say that there are some problems with *Signor* Duccio."

The young man shook his head and said, " We have nothing but the highest respect for him. What could be the problem?"

"I am sorry to inform you that the great artist has had a female apprentice working for him for a number of years in a *clandestina* manner…and, well, it is difficult for me to even say the words, but it is thought that Duccio and the girl have been having…relations…after hours at the workshop."

"No! That is hard to believe."

"Well, Bartolomeo, just think back. Do you have a vague memory of seeing one of Duccio's apprentices going back and forth from the shop… wearing a faded orange tunic with a hood pulled down to her eyes?"

"Well, maybe, maybe, I haven't paid too much attention."

Olivetti continued, "I regret to say that since this person is a girl, and she lives in my *contrada,* I have been an eyewitness to the young female coming home alone on several occasions in the evenings without a chaperone."

"That's not right. And are you sure she is an apprentice for Duccio?"

"I saw her in the shop with what I think is a mortar and a---pis."

"Pestle, Corporal, a pestle. That could make me angrier than anything. Some of us young men are married and have children to feed…like me…and we can't find jobs or apprenticeships. If Duccio has been paying a woman instead of us to apprentice for him…well, that's just despicable!"

"As an official with the responsibility of upholding high moral behavior, I just felt I had an obligation to inform you about this. Just imagine if all of our workshop masters conducted business like that!"

Bartolomeo shook his head and muttered, "I still can't believe that Duccio did the other thing though. I always thought that he and Taviana got along well."

Olivetti shook his head and then slowly pulled something out of the pouch on his side and put it into Bartolmeo's hand.

"What is this?" Bartolomeo asked.

Olivetti whispered, "Enough to feed you and your family for a week. There will be more if you can remember…if called upon…to say that you witnessed a girl with Duccio in his office …after the candle blew out."

Bartolomeo was quiet for a moment. Then he said, "I'll challenge my memory," although he still felt somewhat upside-down by all he had heard.

CHAPTER 20

JULY 22, 1311

It wasn't easy for Corporal Olivetti to wake up. His legs were still sore from the day before. However, he was determined to make his way to the hospital to call upon Father Giacobi. He said to himself, *These long walks up and down our cobblestone streets have got to stop. We have to teach Duccio a lesson as soon as possible.*

When Olivetti arrived at the hospital's busy entrance, he was greeted by the same receptionist as usual and implored the man to see his priest, because he said he was fraught with trouble. After what felt like an eternity for Olivetti, Father Giacobi appeared.

"*Buon giorno*, Corporal, I am sorry to inform you that I am very busy right now. The Hospital is full of travelers. One is in the throes of death, and I must give him his last rites. A couple of others are desperately ill and need someone to pray with them."

"*Peccato!*" Olivetti groaned. "How about me---I am a weary traveler."

"*Sì,* but you live within our city walls, and you do not look quite like you're near to leaving this earth. How about if I come to see you tomorrow at your tower…say after the second morning bells ring and people have left for work?"

His head drooped slightly as Olivetti replied, "*Sì, Padre,* but I am very disappointed. I have some very important information for you."

CHAPTER 21

JULY 23, 1311

Just as he promised---on the next day after the second morning bell---Giacobi knocked on Olivetti's door. Following a short inquiry as to one another's well-being, they began their discussion.

"Well, what do you have?" asked the priest.

The corporal put both of his hands behind his back---which looked a little unusual to the priest---and then he crossed his fingers. Olivetti went by the superstition that crossed fingers would protect a liar.

He began, "I met a young man who was out of work and stands outside a lot. He lives right across the *via* from Duccio. I struck up a conversation with him…his name is Bartolomeo…I made inquiry of Bartolomeo as to whether he saw anything unusual going on…"

"And what did this Bartolomeo tell you?" asked Giacobi.

"Well, I described to him what Elisabetta wears everyday and urged him to recall if he had seen her coming back and forth to work at Duccio's."

Giacobi furrowed his brow as he suspected that the corporal may have prompted Bartolomeo to divulge information that he really did not remember.

"Eventually Bartolomeo recalled that he had seen this apprentice and that he had actually witnessed her leaving Duccio's workshop alone at dusk."

"Corporal, that is no more information than you have already presented to *Signor* Lippi."

"Ah, but this is the new and important part, Father. As he mulled on the situation for some time, Bartolomeo remembered that he saw the girl with Duccio after the other apprentices left and that she stayed after the candles went out. Then he saw her rushing out of the shop an hour or so later with her tunic and hood in disarray..."

Giacobi's mouth worked into a frown, and he sighed. "I am suspicious that you put words into this young man's mouth. He is unemployed, correct?"

"*Si.*"

"Did you happen to… to…pay him off to come up with this?"

Olivetti squeezed his crossed fingers extra hard and objected, "I would never do such a thing!"

Olivetti added, "Bartolomeo implied that he would act as a witness for what looked like…like adultery…at Duccio's workshop."

Upon releasing his fingers from their crossed position, the corporal beckoned the priest to make plans to go with him as soon as possible to file a complaint against Duccio for adultery.

What have I gotten myself into? The priest asked himself.

CHAPTER 22

JULY 25, 1311

This cassone is turning out quite well, thought Duccio. It was a simpler one than he had made for the city records---partly because he wasn't getting paid for it and partly because he had to move on to work on his Massa Marittima commission. As his beloved Taviana would say, "We do need to eat and pay our bills."

On the longer sides of the *cassone,* Duccio painted several scenes of people relaxing in the countryside. On one side of the rectangular box, Duccio added a simple portrait of the Madonna and on the other a scene of the boy Jesus in the temple. Inside the *cassone,* he put a small picture on wood panel that he had painted himself.

Then Duccio called to Mimmo across the room, "Mimmo, *per favore* come over here so that I can give you some directions for delivering this *cassone.*"

"*Certo, Signore,*" Mimmo said as he approached the chest. "It's *magnifico*! Elisabetta will love it."

Then Duccio instructed him: "First, go down two doors and see Barbarino. You remember that he has the ox that we used for the installation of the Maestà?"

"Ask him if, for a small fee, we can use his ox and cart to deliver this *cassone*. If and when he gives his consent, you will have the responsibility of delivering it to Elisabetta."

Mimmo muttered a quick *"Sì, sì, Signore,"* immediately put down the brushes he was cleaning, and ran out of the shop to talk with Barbarino.

⊰⊱✳⊰⊱

Duccio and Mimmo loaded the *cassone* onto the oxcart. Elisabetta's father also assisted. He put on the hinges for the *cassone*, and then the plan was for Arnolfino to accompany Mimmo so that he could help unload the *cassone* and bring it into the house. All of this was to be a surprise for Elisabetta.

Mimmo got up on the driver's seat and snapped the whip (albeit ever so lightly) to get the ox going. The ox agreed, and they departed for Elisabetta's.

When they arrived at the home, Anna greeted Mimmo again but this time more receptively than in the past. Arnolfino had told her about the secret, and Anna thought Elisabetta would be delighted with the gift.

"Come in, come in," said Anna.

When Elisabetta saw Mimmo standing there with her father, she could not restrain herself. She came up to him and quickly put both arms around him while still keeping him at a distance. "It is so nice to see you again, Mimmo."

Mimmo's normally olive skin turned a light shade of pink, and he said, "It is so nice to see you too."

Then Mimmo collected himself and announced, "I have a surprise for you fresh from the workshop of Duccio di Buoninsegna, the most renowned artist in all of Siena!"

At that moment, Mimmo opened the door widely, stepped out, engaged the help of Elisabetta's father, and hauled in the *cassone*.

Elisabetta was speechless. She walked around the *cassone* with her mouth open and her hand gently touching the wood. Finally she said, "Oh my…the paintings on the wood panel are so lovely." And when she opened the cover, she stared with eyes wide open at the little painting Duccio had made for her. It was an angel. Actually, it was one of the faces of the Maestà angels for which she had posed.

Elisabetta had shared the secret of the angels recently with her mother, and so Anna said with a tear in her eye, "This is so *meraviglioso*! Someday you can share this picture with your children and grandchildren, and they will know that you were one of Duccio's angels...or, I should say, all of Duccio's angels."

"I imagine that this is a message as a well as a gift from *Signor* Duccio," said Elisabettta. "He wants me to...to... start thinking about the future, about marriage and a family. I have heard of these new...I think they are called "hope chests"."

Mimmo interjected, "*Signor* Duccio also thought you could store your own small paintings in the chest to keep them as your hidden treasure."

"You must have noticed those paintings in the corner, Mimmo. I will keep them in my chest, but when I think about getting married it could only be to a man who appreciates my art ...or at least does not rebuke it."

CHAPTER 23

JULY 26, 1311

It was a regular morning mass. The priest broke the bread as he looked at the altarpiece ahead of him. The community of believers and monks exchanged their usual liturgical chants. The thurible containing incense was swung over the altar. The sights, smells, and sounds of the mass were all as they should be.

But then something happened that wasn't as it should be. Quiet talking and giggling were occurring behind the altar. *This is completely unacceptable*, Father Giacobi thought, and he had to exercise all of his willpower to keep from running behind the altar and berating the offenders.

Within a few minutes after the disturbance began, mass was over.

Giacobi rushed towards the rear of the altarpiece to find eight little children coming from behind the altar. It was the Latroba and Manelli children.

Signor Latroba spoke quickly, "We were kneeling in the first row here and in such deep prayer that we did not notice that our young ones snuck away from us." He turned to his children and shouted, "You will be in big trouble when you get home, children!"

The little ones looked down and actually seemed surprised that they did something wrong. One of them said, "But, *Papà*, we just wanted to look at the back and see where Grandfather was. We heard that he was *Santo Pietro* and he was!"

Now *Signor* Manelli addressed the children: "Listen, all of you, you had no...no right to disturb the mass." Then the *Signore* turned to Father Giacobi and said, "Believe me, Father, this will never happen again."

Signor Latroba added his certitude to the matter.

Finally Father Giacobi smiled and said, "The altar of God is a holy place, and..." Patting one of the children on the head, he said, "Perhaps the back of the altar...with pictures of relatives and neighbors... is just...just too much temptation for you." Then he crossed himself as he said to all "Go in peace."

<hr />

That evening for their prearranged visit, Father Giacobi all but flew across the Commune to Olivetti's tower. The corporal was the surprised one this time when he saw the other man's appearance.

"Father, you are frowning...you're out of breath... What's wrong?"

"I am ready to go along with your plan of having the so-called witness testify. And I am going to add one more part that I think will really get the Council of Nine's attention."

"Pray tell," said Olivetti.

"The Anonymous Denouncer's Box is located at the Palazzo Pubblico. I imagine you are familiar with it. It's actually the opening to the mouth of the lion sculpture in the front hallway. I am going to ask one of the monks to put a note in it for me."

"Yes?"

"Something happened today that convinced me for once and for all that we must do something about the back of the Maestà."

"What happ…"

"I don't want to discuss it. I just know we have to act. The note is going to accuse Duccio of…of…treason."

"*Ahi*, that's a big accusation."

"This afternoon I got to thinking, and I believe that Duccio's true loyalties may be with the Guelphs in Florence and not our Ghibellines in Siena."

"How could Duccio side with those Guelphs who want the pope to run our region? How could he not see that the Holy Roman Emperor would be a much better leader?"

Olivetti sat quietly for a while and then said, "That explains why he didn't muster with our troops or attend our meetings."

The priest continued, "Remember how he got the commission to do that Madonna painting in Florence? It could very well have been given to any of Florence's very prestigious painters like Cimabue or Giotto…then I vaguely remember that Duccio stayed in Florence for several weeks to install the painting. How long does it take to do something like that?"

"What led you to think that he was in Florence for a few weeks?"

Father Giacobi stuttered a little. "I have my sources," he finally said. He knew he could not break the confidentiality agreement between priest and penitent. In this case, Taviana had come to confession years ago and had admitted anger with her husband because he had been gone for several weeks in Florence.

Olivetti recalled something. "You may remember that neighbor of Duccio's …I think his name is Ignazio…the man who recently ran out of town before having to stand trial for treachery. The heralds kept announcing that people should be on the lookout for him."

"What about him?"

"Duccio used to associate with Ignazio at the *taverna*. At least that's what some *contrade* officers told me."

"Ah, that is another form of proof that could be given for Duccio's sympathy with the Guelphs," said Giacobi.

After a pause, Olivetti said, "Then, this is what I think we should do. First, I will go to the Council of the Nine with my eyewitness proof about the adultery and then a couple of days later you put your treason charge into the Anonymous Denouncer's Box. That should really get the Council's attention!"

PART FIVE

AUGUST 2-25, 1311

CHAPTER 24

AUGUST 2, 1311

Duccio woke up later than usual. *Grazie a Dio*, he said to himself. *Taviana is at mass and won't know I overslept.* He threw on his leggings and tunic and went downstairs to prepare for his day's work. He began studying his preliminary sketches for the Massa Marittima Maestà, but feared that they were uninspired. Duccio thought, *Ever since things have been going well I have lost my muse Obsession. I thought Obsession was my enemy, but maybe she has been my friend.*

All of a sudden, he heard Bang, Bang, Bang---a loud pounding on his workshop door. It could not be Mimmo. He definitely had a gentler touch.

Duccio opened the door and there in front of him stood two large men dressed in the bright colors of the Palazzo Pubblico messengers. These visitors had appeared at his doorstep before, and it had never been pleasant. The men asked to enter. Duccio felt he had no choice but to let them come in. He sat down on a short wooden stool to brace himself for what was coming next.

One of the two said loudly, "We come from the magistrate's office to summons you to appear before the magistrate at the Palazzo Pubblico in one month --- on September first in the year of thirteen eleven--- to answer charges of adultery and perfidy."

The messenger marched forward to hand Duccio the parchment with the summons. Duccio grabbed the summons out of his hand and yelled, "Get out, get out of my house and never come back again!" Both messengers turned on their heels as one and marched out of the workshop with their heavy boots thumping loudly.

Where is this coming from? Duccio asked as he looked down and kicked the floor. He knew he had not committed adultery. He also knew that he was not guilty of treason. He balled up the parchment and threw it across the room.

At that very moment, Taviana opened the door and said, "Hello, *mio sposo*, how are…you don't look good."

Duccio could only gesture to the balled-up piece of paper he had thrown a couple of yards from him. Slowly, Taviana went to pick it up and look at its contents, although she did not know how to read.

She brought it to Duccio and said, "I have seen papers like this from the Commune before, and they have never been good."

Duccio sat with his head in his hands, and so Taviana asked, "What did you do now? What does this paper say?"

He would have preferred sitting on a hundred pins and needles to revealing the contents of the summons to Taviana, but he knew he must. Also, he felt blameless for both of the offenses of which he was accused.

"It says here that I am accused of…of… adultery… and perfidy but gives no further details."

Taviana looked at Duccio with new eyes. "Have you been seeing…or doing things with… another woman?"

"*Dio*, no. You know I love you alone, and I feel so…thankful…to you for…everything…everything… I have no idea where this adultery charge is coming from."

Taviana started sobbing and breathing irregularly. "But then why…why would anyone make these charges?"

Duccio could only shake his head and hold back his own tears.

"And what is perf...?" Taviana couldn't say the word that was so foreign to her.

"Perfidy is a term that accuses a person of being disloyal to his or her own country." Duccio paused for a moment and spit out the words, "It could go so far as to say a person is a spy giving out secrets to an enemy..."

Taviana started shaking her head now as she was sobbing, "That is probably all of Olivetti's doing... from you not attending the musters." She paused and took a deep breath and then said, "But you're an old man, and you haven't gotten into trouble for any of those militia things for...at least...the last five or six years."

"I don't know, I don't know. Maybe they think now...now... that I am brewing up trouble in the background. The only one who would have made up those perfidy charges is that thick-headed Corporal Olivetti. But I don't know about these adultery charges..."

Taviana pulled up a stool next to Duccio's and took his hand.

Duccio decided what to do. "I will go to the Palazzo Pubblico tomorrow and...I will see one of the Council of the Nine and see if he will tell me what these charges are all about." He forced a smile for Taviana and said, "Perhaps someone just made a mistake."

Taviana slowly began breathing more regularly. Duccio tightened his hand on hers, but then she got up and walked towards the stairs, "I love you, *mio sposo*," she said, "I hope that there has been some mistake, but...but...I can't pretend that I am all right."

As Taviana climbed the stairs to retire to their living quarters, Duccio's chest heaved deeply. *Perhaps the omen of the pierced finger is creating this bad luck even though a whole two months has gone by... Things were just going too well for me... I am back to my bad luck.*

CHAPTER 25

AUGUST 3, 1311

Father Giacobi was in the priest's private prayer chapel at the hospital. He did not know whether Duccio had received his charges of adultery and perfidy yet, but, if not, the summons would be coming soon.

The priest tried to pray, but he didn't know how to begin. He thought, *I finally know what the people in my flock feel like. It is so hard to know what is right or wrong. Up until now, all of my decisions have been made for me, and it has been easy to obey my superiors like a good sheep.*

Finally the words stumbled from the priest's heart: "Dear Father in heaven, please forgive me if I have made the wrong choice, but I've done what I have done for you.

Lord, when you have gazed upon the back of the Maestà where Duccio depicts Sienese buildings and even the black and white insignia of Siena on the gate where Jesus enters Jerusalem…Well, don't you think that could make our people become too puffed up? …like the Babylonians who built the big tower that You destroyed with all of the people in it.? Considering all of the new wealth and glory that Siena has been getting, couldn't this happen?

And again, as I have said to you before, Lord, it seems like Duccio is making almost a joke of your followers when he depicts them with the faces of our ordinary citizens. You've seen how people have been coming to the Cathedral looking for depictions of their friends and relatives in the holy scenes on the back of the Maestà. If I am around, I chastise them when they laugh. Even though a couple of the other priests say that attendance at the masses has grown a little, this isn't the way to bring in worshippers, is it, Lord?

Maybe I am trying to convince myself that I have done the right thing…I hope Duccio doesn't suffer too much. I can only hope you approve."

The priest paused a little and then said Amen with more of a sigh than an exclamation. He slowly got up from his kneeling position, wiped a few tears from his eyes, and dragged himself to the interior of the hospital to give comfort to the sick and dying.

Duccio left Mimmo in charge. Then he limped to the Palazzo.

These cobblestones feel unusually hard and bumpy today, thought Duccio. *What a difference a day makes. To think that just a month or so ago I felt like a young man walking back and forth to my vineyard.*

Upon arriving at the Palazzo, Duccio found his way to the reception area for the Council of Nine, The clerk gave him a smile, but Duccio did not return it.

"I'd like to see *Signor* Lippi this morning," said Duccio as he barely spat out the words.

The clerk responded, "And who shall I say is wishing to see him?"

"Duccio di Buoninsegna," he responded dully.

"Oh, *Signore*, we in Siena appreciate so much the beautiful Maestà you made for our Cathedral. I feel so close to the Holy Mother and Jesus every time I go to mass now."

"That's well and good, but I need to see *Signor* Lippi as soon as possible."

With head down a little now, the clerk said, "I will get *Signor* Lippi immediately…if he is free."

Duccio hardly had a moment to take a seat before Lippi came out of his office to see him. "*Signor* Duccio, please come in. It is such an honor to have the pleasure of your acquaintance."

No response came from Duccio. As he just about threw his summons onto Lippi's desk, Duccio said, "Let's dispense with the small talk, *Signor* Lippi. Your name is on this piece of paper. You are being so respectful to me now… yet you sent me this summons accusing me of things I have never done. This is…this is rubbish!"

"All right, *Signor* Duccio, I will dispense with the small talk, but I do admire your artistry. Let's look at this." A pause ensued.

"Yes…I regret to say…that on the first charge a witness said he saw you two times in your office at dusk… with a girl. According to the witness, you let the candle go out…but the girl remained…for now, you know, this is all hearsay, *Signore*… but the witness does accuse you of…of… adultery."

"Who is this witness making this ridiculous charge?"

"Oh, we must keep that confidential until we have the preliminary hearing."

Duccio gritted his teeth. "And who does this so-called witness say that I supposedly committed adultery with?"

"The witness names the girl as…" Lippi thumbed through his papers. "As Elisabetta Buccini, the carpenter's daughter."

"*Uffa,*" Duccio groaned.

Duccio remembered that Elisabetta had stayed until dusk a few times to pose for his angels, but she never stayed long enough for Duccio to even have to light a candle, and her brother had always escorted her home--- or so he thought.

Duccio retorted, "I can explain that…"

"*Grazie, Signor* Duccio, but you will have ample opportunity to explain in court."

Duccio took slow deep breaths and closed his eyes slightly as he asked, "And, pray tell, what is the reason for the perfidy charge?"

"An individual used the Anonymous Denouncer's Box…"

"An individual without any courage…"

"Regardless, he accuses you of secretly working with the Guelphs from Florence against us Ghibellines from Siena."

"And what is this coward's reason for the accusation?"

Lippi thumbed through his notes again and said, "The accuser said you stayed in Florence for more than an adequate amount of time when you installed a Madonna painting and that you conspired with your neighbor Ignazio to let spies into our city."

Duccio kicked the empty chair next to him, rose and said, "No one loves Siena more than me…"

Lippi rose also and said, "You will have your day in court to respond at length to these charges. It will probably all work out fine." Lippi smiled slightly.

"*Sì*, it is just a shame that it has to get to that level before I can defend myself in any way."

"I understand…and I would…I would really love to talk with you about the Maestà someday."

Duccio turned and, despite his aching back, walked away standing as straight and strong as he could. He almost laughed as he thought, *Just a couple of months ago I would have swooned to get the praise for my art that I got today.*

❦

On Duccio's way home from the Palazzo, he was surprised by something. *My body does not ache quite as much as when I left home this morning. At least now I know more about the charges. And that helps me feel that perhaps I can defend myself. It's the "not knowing" that will kill a man.*

As he walked further, Duccio thought, *Strange, but this is giving me food for thought about the Massa Marittima Maestà. Now, I can identify with Christ---the sinless victim hanging on the cross… I think that I will give glory to the not-guilty Christ by using thin slivers of fine gold to depict his helpless body hanging on the tree.*

By the time Duccio arrived home, he was deep in thought and even caught himself whistling a little tune. Mimmo knew nothing of why Duccio had gone to the Palazzo, and so he greeted him with a cheerful *"Buon giorno."* Duccio just gave Mimmo a little wave and then climbed the stairs, because he knew Taviana would be pulling her hair out waiting for his report.

"And…?" Taviana looked up at him from the bed on which she was sitting and twirling its straw around her fingers.

"First, the adultery charge. Some witness got the wrong impression that Elisabetta was staying here after hours and that the candle blew out on a couple of occasions…"

Taviana winced and let out a small sharp cry.

"Believe me, Taviana. That did not happen! Second, the perfidy charge. Some cowardly worm put a note in the Anonymous Denouncer's box saying that I stayed longer than needed in Florence when I put in the Madonna piece and that I was somehow conspiring with Ignazio…conspiring, I guess, to overthrow our government…of all things. *Dio mio!*"

"Terribile," cried Taviana.

"Perhaps I can get a lawyer, Taviana. I have heard that the University of Bologna has a fine law school and perhaps…"

"No, Duccio, we cannot do that."

"Why not?"

"We have just come out of debt for the tenth time or so and are able to put food on the table again. We cannot afford a lawyer!"

Duccio had to laugh just a little. "Well, look at you! You are usually the model, gracious Sienese wife, but I think you just put me in my place…and… you …you know what?... I kind of liked it."

Taviana had to chuckle herself even though it was the slightest of chuckles.

CHAPTER 26

AUGUST 10, 1311

After informing Duccio via messenger about their upcoming arrival, a priest and one of the city council members from Massa Marittima came to Duccio's workshop to talk with him about the progress of their Maestà. Duccio shook their hands and led them into his little office.

Signor Moretti began, "I see in your office some sketches here for a Maestà. Does this happen to be for ours?"

"*Sì, Signor* Moretti, yours is the only Maestà I am working on."

The councilman continued, "It appears that you have been doing a lot of work on the Crucifixion scene for the back."

With blue eyes flashing, Duccio leaned forward to them and said, "I want to depict Jesus on the cross at an angle. My wish is to have him stand out as a slender, solitary figure. The land on which the cross stands will look barren and desolate."

He continued, "The few followers mourning over Jesus' situation will be shown as shadows lying in the crevasses of the landscape. The sky will be a foreboding gray-brown hue to reflect the sadness of the situation, but it will be laced through with slim, brilliant slivers of gold to herald the imminent glory of the risen Lord."

Father Francis pressed Duccio further. "I don't know if Jesus himself should just look slim and solitary. That just sounds so…so…bleak."

"You are right, Father Francis. I neglected to tell you that I would have those thin slivers of gold also running through Christ's body to accentuate His dignity in the face of suffering."

Then Father Francis added, "And, *Signor* Duccio, far be it from me to tell such an outstanding artist as you what to do…but I…well we…would like you to make the people in this Maestà not to look like anyone we know in Massa Marittima."

Duccio chuckled to himself thinking that they must have talked with Father Giacobi. "Oh…all right…If you wish, I can borrow features from my other models, combine them differently, and come up with new faces that wouldn't look like anyone in particular."

"*Si*," said *Signor* Moretti. "That sounds perfect."

"And we are now here also to give you twenty gold florins to purchase your supplies and hire an apprentice to aid you, if need be."

"Twenty gold florins will be adequate to make a beginning. Seeing as how this is a relatively small altarpiece, I believe I can handle it myself at this point. I will request by messenger when I am in need of further funds for an assistant or anything else… Is that acceptable?"

The patrons found that very acceptable and left with smiles and hand-shakes. Duccio sat back and said to himself, *It is amazing how one man like Father Giacobi can block change and innovation. News of his disdain must have spread to these good men. Ah well, so be it.*

Duccio climbed the stairs to share the results of the meeting with Taviana. "I have good news, *mia sposa*. We will not be going hungry any time soon. I have received twenty gold florins as an initial payment from our guests."

Taviana was cutting beets and carrots on their oak table, and her usually decisive cutting hand was shaking somewhat, "*Bene, bene*, but I am still worried ---perhaps I should say frantic---about how this court case is going to turn out. We only have two weeks until the first hearing."

Duccio walked over to her, slowly took the knife out of her hand, and ushered her to a bench where he sat next to her. "You and I have successfully kept these charges a secret. So, no disgrace has fallen on us yet. Perhaps a miracle will happen or someone will recognize an error…but I have to admit that I am very concerned about how this might look for you and Elisebetta if these ridiculous adultery charges continue…"

Taviana's beet-stained hand took Duccio's, and she said, "I am more worried about you. If they find you guilty of committing adultery, that will mean the usual seven lashes with a whip in the piazza in front of our whole Commune. That would be so embarrassing to you, and your old body might not be able to take it…"

Duccio made a large false frown and said, "Taviana. Are you implying that I am an old man?"

Then he laughed, and a small smile escaped from Taviana.

However, later that evening Duccio scolded their grandson, "Giovanni, you are chewing too loudly…and quit kicking the table leg!" This was not like Duccio, and then he proceeded to drink two goblets of wine in quick succession.

Shortly thereafter when Angelina and the children retired to their sleeping area Duccio picked up his cloak and pulled it around his shoulders. Taviana went to Duccio's side and roughly tried to pull off his cloak. She looked him in the eye and said, "Do not go out tonight, *mio marito*. I know that when you have tension you like to go out and talk with people at the *taverna*. But tonight, you cannot do it!"

"Why not? I feel like my skin is crawling."

"Why not? Because with a couple of more goblets of wine you will spill everything about what's going on with the court, and then we will really be miserable tomorrow. We...we...can get out a cask of our best wine from your vineyard, and you can drink to your heart's content...but you must... you must...do it here."

Duccio looked back into her eyes, slunk down on the bench and said, "You are right, *mia sposa*, you are right."

CHAPTER 27

AUGUST 11, 1311

Father Giacobi was hard at prayer in the priest's little chapel. As usual in the last couple of months, he briefly interceded for the sick and dying, but then he would return to trying to convince himself and God that he was doing the right thing in the Maestà matter.

While the priest was at prayer, a sweat-covered, disheveled man entered the hospital and asked Brother Matteo at the door, "May I please see Father Giacobi right away? It is a very serious matter."

"I am sorry, *Signore*, but Father is praying…"

"But if you know what this is about, you will understand my sense of urgency."

Matteo proceeded to listen to the man and immediately ran to the chapel.

"Father Giacobi, I apologize for interrupting your prayer, but your brother is in the reception area and needs to speak with you about a…a…vital matter."

Immediately, Father Giacobi got up from his bended knees and hastened to the reception area to find which brother had come to see him.

When he saw that it was his brother Galgano and looked at his face, he said, "Dear Galgano, what brings you here in such distress?"

"May I speak with you in private, Giacobi?"

"*Certo, certo*, come to my quarters." The priest knew that he could only see family members twice a year and that his sister from Siena had just come to visit a couple of months ago. However, he felt that whatever news Galgano was carrying would be an exception that God would understand.

Wincing at how his brother's room was so small and stark, Galgano began, "I don't know how you live like this after our years in the open fields…"

"I am content, Galgano, please…"

"All right, Giacobi, I might as well tell you straight out. Our father and mother were working in the vineyard…just doing some simple chores and…"

"*Per favore*, Galgano, just get to the point. What happened?"

"Father started breathing hard, he held his heart, he fell to the ground, and he just looked up at mother who was cradling his head in her arms. He couldn't say anything. Then he just quit breathing…. with his eyes wide open… still staring at our mother."

"*Terribile!*" Giacobi yelled out. He plopped down on his bed and put his head into his hands.

Galgano sat next to him and slowly put his arm around his brother. "This happened a day and a half ago. Mother sent me here to tell you and the rest of the family in Siena. We are all so…sad."

"I feel devastated," said the priest between sobs. "Father was always so good to us…I wish I could have said goodbye to him…I have only seen him four or five times since I took my vows…"

Galgano did not know what to say. He just tightened his hold on his brother's shoulder and pulled him closer.

After some time of weeping and consoling one another, Father Giacobi rose, straightened his robe and asked Galgano, "Has Mother considered arrangements for…it is so hard to say this…burying our father?" and tears escaped from him again.

"Mother says she wants to have our father buried in the cemetery near our church in the village. She would like you to come and say the mass for Father…she wants our whole family and a few friends to be together for it."

"I will arrange to do that."

After breaking the news to his brother and sister, Galgano set forth to the home and workshop of Duccio di Buoninsegna. Galgano's mother had instructed him to make certain that he contact Duccio, especially since he was the owner of the vineyard and would want to know about this turn of events.

When Galgano walked through the open workshop door, he was greeted by Mimmo who then brought him to Duccio's office.

"*Buon giorno*, Galgano. So nice to see you ag…" Duccio began, but when he saw the man's changed appearance he knew this was not a social call.

"Sit, sit, Galgano. What is on your mind?"

Galgano's lips quivered. Tears welled in his eyes, and he said, "*Signor* Duccio, I have bad news. I don't know how to tell you in any other way. So, I will just tell you… my father is dead."

"*Dio mio!*" Duccio exclaimed loudly. "Why, I was just visiting him and your family about a month ago at the vineyard. What…what happened?"

When Taviana heard Duccio cry out, she came down the stairs. "What, what has happened now?"

"Taviana, this is Galgano, the son of Luca. You haven't been to the vineyard for a long time. So, you probably don't remember him."

"No, I'm sorry, I don't."

"Galgano, could you continue with…"

"I am sorry to tell you, *Signora*, but my father, Luca Constanzi, your husband's vintner…has…has passed away."

"*Terribile!*" gasped Taviana.

"I was telling *Signor* Duccio how he passed…he just died suddenly in the vineyard…while my mother cradled him in her arms." Galgano said, as he gained some comfort from the repetition.

"This saddens me greatly," Duccio said. "Your father was a great man. He handled the vineyard so well, but he was also…kind…and good…"

"I know, *Signore,* I know. My mother asked me if you would be so gracious as to attend his funeral mass at our humble country church…and she knows you may have some questions about the vineyard…since my father is gone…"

"I will be at the mass," said Duccio with his head hung low.

CHAPTER 28

AUGUST 14, 1311

Mourners entered the Mary Queen of Heaven country church in which Luca's casket was displayed. Rosa had to be physically aided by her children to a bench in the front right aisle facing the altar. Her five children and eleven grandchildren took up the next two rows of chairs and benches that neighbors had scurried to find to put into the church for the funeral.

Father Giacobi had his back to the mourners as he prayed aloud at the altar with the small wooden crucifix on it. Then he turned to the people and said, "My good father will most certainly go to heaven, because he believed in Jesus and honored the Holy Mother…"

At that moment, Father Giacobi noticed a familiar-looking man quietly entering the church. The man looked tired, perhaps even haggard, but his clothes were the type worn in the city and not in the country. As the priest continued his address, he realized that the latecomer was none other than Duccio di Buoninsegna!

What brings that man here! Giacobi exclaimed to himself.

He continued with his pre-planned homily---as best he could---with his heart beating doubly hard and tension enveloping his body. He trembled, partly out of love for his father and partly because of the appearance of the man about whom he had prayed so much.

Rosa turned to one of her children and said, "Giacobi loved his father so much. You see how he is shaking."

Never before had the priest been so relieved to give the final benediction.

⌗

After the service, family and friends sojourned to the little *casa* that Rosa, two of her sons, and her grandchildren now inhabited---without Luca. The house was not large enough for all of the mourners. So most sat or stood outside. The guests brought fresh fruit, olives, vegetables, meats, and, of course, the best of wine.

When he entered the *casa* with his mother. Father Giacobi quietly but sharply whispered to her, "What is Duccio, the painter, doing here?"

Seeing no reason to whisper, Rosa answered in a normal tone, "Did you not know that *Signor* Duccio owns this vineyard?"

"*Dio mio!*" said the priest.

With a little laugh, Rosa asked, "Now, Giacobi, are you taking God's name in vain? Let me bring you over to where *Signor* Duccio is standing outside and perhaps you two can exchange greetings."

Rosa grabbed her son's hand and pulled him to where Duccio was standing and talking with a couple of field hands who worked in the vineyard.

When Duccio saw the priest, he said, "I am so sorry about your father… it was so sudden."

"*Si.*"

"He was a wonderful man and so good at managing the vineyard…"

"*Si,*" said Father Giacobi as he thought, *Duccio probably has no idea that I was behind the perfidy charge. Thank God!*

Father Giacobi regained his voice, "Ah, how was your journey here, *Signore?* Did you ride or walk?"

"I got a few *soldi* together and rented a horse, Father."

'Well…nice talking with you *Signor* Duccio…I need to talk with my uncle over there who I haven't seen for years. Can you excuse me, *Signor* Duccio?"

"*Certo.*"

❧❊❧

As the sun was beginning to set, almost all of the visitors left. Duccio remained. Rosa urged him not to ride his rented horse back at dusk because of the many stories she had heard of people being robbed and beaten on the road to Siena---especially when darkness was descending. Duccio wanted to stay anyhow, because he knew he had to discuss business with the family--- even though he wished it could wait.

The *casa* was crowded with the immediate family---including Father Giacobi who had taken off his monastic robe and donned Galgano's old tunic and leggings. Soon after the children went to bed, Duccio began, "Luca was the best vintner and person that a man could have working for him."

All eyes were on Duccio, and no one stirred.

"I must now make a decision as to where the vineyard will go next."

"Sandro, I got to know you on my last trip here. Galgano, you were working in the fields then, but you were kind enough to handle the difficult job of breaking the news to all of us in Siena about your father."

"I'd like to know if either… or both of you know how to choose the best grapes and make them into the wine…and does one or both of you know how to keep records of what is bought and sold for an owner to look at?"

Sandro and Galgano looked at each other.

Galgano answered first: "*Signore*, I am good with numbers. Father taught me how to write down our trans….transactions. I can even spell the simple words we need to record things that are bought and sold."

"*Bene, bene*, Galgano, that's very *importante*, but it's not e…"

"*Signore*, I pride myself on planting and reaping the best grapes in all of Toscana," Sandro declared.

Rosa added, "*Signore*, these two sons of mine have loved working with their dear father…" Then she began weeping and could not continue.

Her daughters rushed to her side, patted her hands and put their arms around her shoulders.

Father Giacobi stared hard at Duccio. He thought, *What will he do? This will show the true makings of the man.*

Duccio looked from one family member to another and said, "It pains me that Luca is gone, but I believe that between the two of you---Sandro and Galgano---you have the passion…and…the ability…to do his job."

Together everyone in the room exhaled as one.

Duccio continued, "I hereby make you two brothers the new managers of my vineyard, and your whole family is welcome to remain in this *casa* for as long as I live and own this land."

Rosa pulled herself up and walked to Duccio to grab his hands and say, "*Molte grazie, molte grazie, Signor* Duccio. God will bless you for this!"

Duccio said under his breath, "I am not so sure about that." And then louder he said, "I am glad that this brings some comfort to you and your family, Rosa."

Then Duccio said, "I think I will go outside now and breathe some of your country air that I love so much."

When he walked about twenty paces from the *casa*, he felt a breeze gently gliding through his hair. He heard the hooting of an owl, and he saw the stars twinkling in the sky.

At that moment, Father Giacobi came up to Duccio with a glass of wine for the artist as well as himself.

"*Grazie*," said Duccio. "It is so refreshing, isn't it, to get away from the sound of horses' hoofs clicking on the cobblestones, the smell of the rubbish…"

"*Sì*," said the priest. "Look at the moon to your right, *per favore*. Since I have been in Siena, I have never seen the moon shining so brightly. We rarely even see the moon and stars shining---even dimly--- with all of the smoke in the city…"

"We know we have to obey those bells to put out our fires so that our houses don't burn down in the middle of the night…but…the smoke when we do that is awful, isn't it?" concurred Duccio.

Giacobi replied, "*Si, si.* I used to love to walk in these fields here when I was a boy, but I think I missed some of the best parts of living in the country. I was always so afraid of…getting my hands dirty or skinning my knees."

"*Si*, if we only knew as children what we know now…" Duccio said.

"Later, when I joined the monastery," Giacobi continued, "I thought that the people back home were nice but rather…how shall I say it?…Simple-minded, I guess would be the word."

"*Si*," said Duccio, "Especially when you are taught to read as an apprentice or a priest, you start thinking you're better than others who can't…at least, that's the way I have felt at times."

"But now that I am back among these folk, *Signor* Duccio, I feel that I underestimated them. Perhaps they know how to live…in a way that's better than us city people."

"I know what you are saying, Father. I know what you are saying."

"There's a certain freedom you feel here, isn't there?" mused Giacobi.

Duccio replied, "Over the years when I have left the city walls and viewed the beautiful vineyards, I have always loved it, but I knew I could never be completely happy just contemplating grapes. My mind has always told me that I must paint, and I have to remain in the city to do that."

"And my mind and heart has always told me that I must serve God, and I have always thought that a large cathedral was the place to do it."

Duccio finally took a sip of his wine. "Now I have come to a time in my life when I think the day will come…that I won't mind living in the country, especially with my Taviana, and we can watch the grapes ripen…together."

As the priest indulged in a couple of sips of wine, he responded, "Do you think we can change? I mean, do you think we can live our lives in a different way as we get older?"

"I believe we can," said Duccio. "I believe we can."

CHAPTER 29

AUGUST 15, 1311

On the next day when Duccio rode back to Siena, he realized how difficult the saunter was on his posterior and his back. He thought, *Ach! Old age...Somehow I thought it was something that others---but not me---would fall prey to.*

When he arrived at the outskirts of Siena to drop off his horse, Duccio remembered that this was the first of two days that his fellow Sienese had shuttered their workshops and were celebrating the Assumption of the Virgin. He made his way home through the processions of people carrying statues and icons of Mary. Drenched with sweat, Duccio finally pulled open the door of his workshop. When she heard the door loudly creak open, Taviana came downstairs. Even though it was a holiday for people of the Commune, Mimmo had come to the workshop to do some simple cleanup jobs.

"I am so happy to see you again, *mio sposo,*" Taviana exclaimed as she came up to Duccio and gave him a hug. "You look like you just finished a jousting match."

"I feel like it too. I will fill you in on the burial and all… after I hear what has been going on here."

Mimmo began. "Two things happened while you were gone." Taviana knew what they were and reverted to wringing her hands--- a new habit that she had recently acquired.

Mimmo continued, "Ambrogio and Simone stopped in for one of their visits. They were so sorry that they missed you, but they dropped off a couple of things."

Kicking off his heavy boots and sitting on a stool next to his wife, Duccio asked, "And what, pray tell, did they leave?"

"They had met after I told them about Elisabetta's…situation…and they decided to each make a small painting for her *cassone*. Isn't that nice? They left them in your office wrapped carefully in cloths."

"All right, I can tell from my the way *mia sposa* is wringing her hands that not all of the news is good. Let's get to the not-so-good thing that happened," Duccio said as he sighed.

"Elisabetta came here herself---with her father. She was crying, and she said something about a summons. Both she and her father were talking about being disgraced. They looked sad…but also…angry."

Taviana looked at Duccio. "She must have got the same summons as you did…finally."

Duccio squeezed Taviana's hand and said, "I will have to take Mimmo aside to explain everything to him." Then he looked at Mimmo and said slowly, loudly and distinctly, "But you must swear to keep this story a secret."

"*Certamente, certamente*," said Mimmo with such seriousness that one would think he was going off to battle against the Florentines.

⚜

Duccio said to Taviana, "First, come with me and look at the paintings that Ambrogio and Simone did. They may cheer us up."

Mimmo returned to his cleaning.

When Duccio saw the paintings in their wrappings on his desk, he chuckled, "It looks like some little mice may have jumped up and played with this cloth to loosen it up."

Taviana had to laugh a little, "Mimmo just couldn't wait until you got home, it looks like."

Duccio unwrapped one and then another. With each one, he exclaimed, "*Stupendo!*" These young men have found their muses, and I am certain that Elisabetta will love these pieces."

"They are indeed special, *mio sposo.* You taught the boys well."

❦

When Duccio told Mimmo the whole story about the adultery and the treachery charges, Mimmo was astounded. "This is so unfair," he had said. "How could anyone accuse you and Elisabetta of such things!"

"The world can be an unfair place," Duccio muttered.

After Mimmo recovered from the shock of the news, Duccio had a request for him. "I am hoping that you will do an errand for me tomorrow... after the Feast Day of the Assumption."

"*Sì,* anything."

"I would like you to deliver Ambrogio and Simone's paintings to Elisabetta. Looking at them should cheer her up."

"There is no doubt that they would," Mimmo replied.

"And feel free to let her know that we have discussed the unfair charges against her...and me. She may need a friend---like you--- to talk with about all of this. Please tell her and her father that no one will be able to prove the... the... accusation against Elisabetta and me, if you would like. And, *per favore,* tell her father that he is welcome to come back and see me if he has more concerns. Got that?"

"I think so," replied Mimmo as he repeated aloud to himself, "Give her the paintings. Tell them there is no proof and that her father can come see you."

CHAPTER 30

AUGUST 16, 1311

Mimmo could hardly wait to do his errand. After the morning work bells rang, he went to Duccio's desk to get the paintings. He tucked one under each arm as if he were carrying two packages of meat home from the market.

When he arrived at Elisabetta's door, he smiled and then knocked loudly. His grin evaporated when Elisabetta's father opened the door and said, "What are you doing here? Anyone having to do with Duccio's workshop is not welcome here."

Elisabetta heard her father addressing Mimmo so curtly and came to the door herself. "*Papà*, please let Mimmo in. He has done nothing wrong…just as *Signor* Duccio has done nothing wrong."

"All right, come in, young man, and tell us what you are here for."

"Mainly, I have brought some gifts for Elisabetta's *cassone*… from Ambrogio and Simone. You remember them from their helping to haul the Maestà to the Cathedral, don't you, *Signor* Buccini?"

Signor Buccini did not answer.

Elisabetta carefully unwrapped the cloths around the gifts, and when she saw the paintings, she said, *"Belle, bellissime!* Wouldn't you know that Ambrogio would paint our townspeople in their daily activities and Simone would depict the Virgin as if on a fine stage!"

"Sì, sì!" agreed Mimmo.

Anna crossed herself when she saw the picture of the Virgin, and Arnolfino looked closely at the neighborhood scene. Elisabetta re-wrapped the pieces and brought them to where her *cassone* was. Her father lifted the heavy cover of the chest, and Elisabetta put the pictures next to her creations.

Mimmo followed her to her *cassone*, and, in so doing, he noticed that Elisabetta had already put some domestic objects into what actually might become her "hope chest." There were embroidered napkins and a box for silverware like one that he had seen his grandmother use.

Since his arrival, the family's spirits had improved so much that Mimmo did not want to deliver the rest of the message from Duccio. He thought, but could not say aloud, *I am glad you are moving on, Elisabetta, but I hope it won't be too far from me.*

While Mimmo was gone, Duccio was deeply involved in his painting of the Crucifixion. All of a sudden, he heard the clamoring of men in heavy boots at his open workshop door.

Duccio hardly blinked. *What more could happen to me? Let it come. Let it come.*

The two men advanced towards Duccio, and one said, "We have another message for you, Duccio di Buoninsegna!"

"Fine, hand it over."

The men delivered their announcement, clicked their boots together, turned as one, and marched off together again.

"How repetitious this is becoming," Duccio said under his breath. "I hope they don't think they are intimidating me anymore."

He slowly unfurled the parchment and read, "The perfidy charge against you, Duccio di Buoninsegna, is hereby cancelled."

This time Duccio did not ball up the letter and throw it into a corner. In fact, he gave it a little kiss and reread the message.

"Taviana, Taviana, I have wonderful news!" He shouted as he bounded up the stairs as fast as he could. "The perfidy charge has been dropped!"

"*Santa Madonna!*" Taviana said as she used the exclamation she reserved for only the most important of occasions.

CHAPTER 31

AUGUST 19, 1311

Duccio and Mimmo started out early for the market to purchase additional gold leaf for the Massa Marittima Maestà. The day was hot, the market was crowded, and the trader who sold gold leaf was not there. Since the Palazzo Pubblico was right there on the piazza where the market was held, Duccio made a suggestion to Mimmo.

"Mimmo, how about if you accompany me to see *Signor* Lippi, one of the Council of Nine magistrates? I'd like to ask him why, Praise the Lord, the perfidy charges were dropped."

"As usual, *Signor* Duccio, I am at your service."

"You know, Mimmo, I have always prided myself on being able to do everything on my own. But, at this time of my life and with the way things have been going… I think I need a shoulder to lean on."

"Really?"

"Really," said Duccio as he put his arm through Mimmo's and held onto him for support.

Mimmo had never experienced the physical touch of Duccio---except in occasional work-related contacts. "I am proud to have your arm through mine," he said.

Walking with a limp, Duccio proceeded with Mimmo through the portico of the Palazzo and then into the hall where one of the first *cassoni* for Siena's records was proudly displayed. "That looks a little like the *cassone* you made for Elisabetta, but it doesn't have your beautiful artwork on it."

"*Sì, sì*, Mimmo, it is an old one. And now let us proceed to the magistrates' reception area and, hopefully, Lippi will be able to see us."

The same receptionist greeted Duccio again, although more quietly than the last time. On this occasion, Duccio was the smiling one.

"And how are you today *Signore?*" asked Duccio. Upon hearing the man's faint reply, Duccio asked to see *Signor* Lippi.

When told that *Signor* Lippi could see him, Duccio responded, "*Molto grazie* and have a nice day." The receptionist could only stare at Duccio and his assistant as they made their way to Lippi's office. He thought, *Is this the same Duccio who refused to talk to me the last time?*

"Greetings," said *Signor* Lippi.

"And greetings to you, *Signore*. I have brought my office assistant, Mimmo, and have come to inquire as to the reason for the good news I received yesterday from your messengers."

"Being one of your greatest admirers, *Signor* Duccio, I was delighted to send the message to you that the perfidy charge has been dropped. You will recall that the accusation was made through the Anonymous Denouncer's slot. Whoever made those charges came back just two days ago and put in a new letter saying he wanted to cancel his accusation. All of us from the Council of Nine got together to compare the first and second letter to see if the handwriting was identical. It was, and that is why we dropped the charges!"

"Did you say charges?" Duccio asked.

"Oh, I am sorry, *Signore*. I misspoke. Just one charge is dropped. The other one remains."

Duccio's shoulders slumped slightly, "I thought that was the case. But I need to prepare myself for all of this. Will the remaining hearing be heard… in private or public?"

"It will be a public hearing, but if you and the accused have not told anyone about the charge, word of the hearing would probably not be spread."

"Well, that is good."

"The only people mandated to appear will be you, the other party…is it Elisabetta?…and the witness making the charge."

"I would love to see who that is," Duccio muttered.

"Oh, also, a clerk will be present who will record what is said and will post the outcome of the hearing on the announcement board that citizens see as they enter the Palazzo."

"Great," Duccio uttered in a low tone.

Then the artist grasped the arms of his wooden chair in order to push himself up. When he stood, Mimmo held his arm out so that Duccio could grab it.

"One charge down and one to go," said Duccio as he stood up as straight as he could. "*Arrivederci, Signor* Lippi. Will I be seeing you in court or is someone else to judge us?"

"Not me, *Signor* Duccio, but I am certain that the man will be quite qualified to grant you a fair hearing. *Arrivederci* to you…and I still love your Maestà."

⚜❊⚜

On his way home from the workshop that day, Mimmo said to himself, *I feel like I could fly but also like I could cry. It was so nice to have Signor Duccio depending on me for a change, but I am so worried that the hearing could bring harm to Elisabetta.*

Mimmo slowly trudged up the stairs to his family's tower but said nothing to his mother as he slumped into the intricately carved chair that was his father's pride. While pulling off his boots, he let out a deep sigh.

"What is wrong, my son?" his mother asked as she finished setting the table for dinner and lighting the candles in their silver holders.

"I have a heavy heart, *Mamma*."

"What, what is it?"

"I don't think I have ever told you that we have had a woman as an apprentice at Duccio's workshop…"

"*Dio, mio*," replied his mother in one of the few times that she took God's name in vain.

Hearing this, Mimmo's father turned from gazing upon the tapestry that he had just bought and hung on the east wall of their domicile. "This sounds *interessante*," he said.

Then Mimmo proceeded to tell his father and mother, Lorenzo and Emilia Androlini, about Elisabetta and the charges against her. Tears filled his eyes at times as Mimmo tried to explain what happened.

Seeing the emotion in their son, Emilia and Lorenzo looked at each other. This was the first time that they had seen their twenty six year old son show strong feelings for a woman. Mimmo was their only child, and his parents had tried to arrange marriages for him with a couple of women, but the transactions were cancelled, because the girl's family could not put up enough of a dowry to please Mimmo's father. Working in the financial office for the Council of Nine for many years, *Signor* Androlini was very business-minded. He and his wife had a beautifully furnished three story tower, but he wanted Mimmo to be set up well also when he got married. However, as hopes dwindled for the perfect arrangement, the Androlinis felt that they would be pleased to have their son matched with any decent girl---even if her family did not have money. Now they just wanted grandchildren to carry on the Androlini name and wanted someone to keep their son warm at night as he crept into old age like them.

"I have to say, *Mamma and Papà*, it would be nice if Elisabetta liked me… as much as I like her."

"Oh, I am sure she does…" his mother began reassuring him.

"But, honestly, I know how people feel about me. People in our *contrada* seem to see me as…as…a little slow."

"Don't say that about yourself," Emilia said again.

"The corporal from our *contrada* doesn't even call me to muster as much as the other fellows. Marching in line with the others…and then fencing… were so hard for me. Corporal Spinnelli told me once he was afraid I could get injured…"

His father interrupted: "But you…you have other strengths, son. For instance, you are such a handsome young man."

Mimmo smiled, "That is true. But I wish I could do as well as I look… Anyhow, that Elisabetta…" Mimmo's eyes drifted off.

Ladling stew from a pot over the fire, his mother said, "Well, let's see if you can eat as well as you look. Let's come together for dinner!"

As they sat down, Lorenzo looked at his wife and thought, *Is it the angle of the sun coming through the window or is it something else that is bringing a twinkle to my wife's eye?*

CHAPTER 32

AUGUST 25, 1311

Duccio and Taviana arrived early for the hearing, as did Elisabetta and her parents. The two sets of people were each seated at their own table, and another table sat empty. Directly in front of the judge's massive wooden desk sat a man with a quill and parchment ready to record the proceedings. Just as the hearing was about to begin, a tall young man entered and was shown by a court worker to the empty table. He snuck a quick look at the people he was accusing and then looked straight ahead.

At that moment, the bailiff said, "All rise," and everyone did.

Garbed in a flowing black robe, the judge walked in. The tall, white-haired man pounded his gavel and said, "You may sit down...Today we have two people accused of adultery---Duccio di Buoninsegna and Elisabetta Buccini. And we have a man named (the judge shuffled his papers)...Bartolomeo Rubino...who is making these charges."

"*Signor* Rubino, would you please come forward and sit in this chair so you may answer my questions."

Bartolomeo slowly rose and walked to the chair that was faced at an angle so the judge could interview him and Bartolomeo could also look the accused in the eyes. He thought to himself, *What am I doing here?* Then he spotted Corporal Olivetti sitting in the back and smiling at him. *I am not sure if that makes me feel better or worse.*

The judge asked, "*Signor* Rubino, what did you witness that caused you to press adultery charges against Duccio di Buoninsegna and Elisabetta Buccini?"

"Your honor, I saw *Signorina* Elisabetta and *Signor Duccio* alone in his work-shop four times when the sun was setting and the apprentices had all left. I gathered that the *Signorina* was also an apprentice hired by Duccio…taking good jobs away from men…" his voice trailed off.

The judge frowned slightly. "It is highly unusual to have a female appren-tice. What proof do you have of that?"

"Well…Corporal Olivetti told me that," said Bartolomeo as he pointed in Olivetti's direction.

The accused and their families sat up straight and quickly turned to see Olivetti sitting in the last row of the room. Olivetti gave a weak smile and slunk down ever so slightly on his bench.

The judge's brow was furrowed now. "How and why did you develop a relationship with Corporal Olivetti?"

Bartolomeo squirmed and beads of sweat appeared on his brow. He did not answer.

The judge said in a louder voice, "I asked you how and why you devel-oped a relationship with Corporal Olivetti."

"I…I…met him when I was standing outside of my building. I lost my job and had nothing else to do. At first, the Corporal warned me about a new problem with thievery in my *contrada*…"

The judge interjected, "So, that is how you started talking. Then what?"

"Then he told me about how Duccio had the gall to hire a female appren-tice when some of us young men can't find work…"

"Yes, the corporal has quite a record of paying attention to other people's business," the judge replied. "But go on, *Signore*, continue."

Now looking pale and answering slowly, Bartolomeo said, "Corporal Olivetti told me that this apprentice lives in his *contrada* and that he had seen her coming home alone at night---without an escort---from Duccio's workshop. Then the corporal got me to think back to the times I …I saw… the girl stay late…in the dark…with candles not being lit. Then I would see the *signorina* scurrying from the workshop. It looked…it looked…like maybe she was ashamed of something."

Taviana winced and slightly kicked Duccio under the desk. Arnolfino looked at his daughter and scowled.

With his hand rubbing his chin, the magistrate sat quietly for a while. He looked at Olivetti and then at the witness: "Did any *soldi* happen to cross hands during your discussions with Corporal Olivetti?"

"Oh, no, *certamente no,*" protested the witness.

"*Grazie, Signor* Rubino. You may step down from the witness seat."

"Now, I call *Signorina* Buccini to approach the chair."

With head slightly bowed, she made her way to the seat,

The judge asked, "And you, young lady, were you really an apprentice to Duccio di Buoninsegna?"

"*Sì,* I begged *Signor* Duccio to let me be his apprentice about eight years ago."

"Could you speak up, *Signorina*? I can hardly hear you."

In a slightly louder voice, Elisabetta said, "*Signor* Duccio was not at all eager for me to be his apprentice, because I was a girl, but…but I told him how much I loved art and painting. He finally gave in."

"How did the other apprentices and patrons of Duccio respond to this?"

"They did not know that I was a girl. I never spoke at the shop. *Signor* Duccio told the others that I was mute. I lowered my hood over my forehead and pretended I was a boy… No one asked any questions."

"That was quite a ruse that you and Duccio pulled off," the judge chuckled. "Now, *Signorina*, I am going to ask you a very difficult question. It is what we are here about. Did you ever have in....intimate ...relations with *Signor* Duccio?"

Now Elisabetta spoke loudly and looked the judge in the eye: "No, your honor, never. There was never anything like that between us. He is a married man. I greatly respect his wife, *Signora* Taviana. I would never do what you are talking about with a man...outside of marriage...his or mine."

"Hmm," the judge cogitated. "You may return to your table, *Signorina*. And now I call *Signor* Duccio to step forward to the witness seat."

Duccio made an effort to stand straight, but he limped to the chair.

"*Signor* Duccio, do you concur with *Signorina* Buccini about why you took her as an apprentice----even though she was a female?"

"Yes, she loved art. I allowed her to enter the shop. She painted beautifully and... she was excellent with the gold leaf."

"But, *Signor Duccio*, was this witness telling a lie that you were with *Signorina* Buccini after work hours alone in your office?"

"No, your honor, he was not lying. What Elisabetta was doing... was... she was posing for the face of my angels in the Maestà. And my wife knew all about it."

The judge stared at Elisabetta for a few seconds and then nodded to himself. Without asking Duccio the same big question he posed to Elisabetta, the judge excused Duccio from his chair and announced to everyone in the courtroom that he would come back with a decision about the adultery charge when the early afternoon bells rang.

⚜

Corporal Olivetti rushed out of the courtroom as quickly as his old legs could take him. He thought, *I will mix in with the people in the piazza, and Duccio and the others from the courtroom will not see me. Oh, how I wish that Bartolomeo would not have mentioned my name. And that judge never did like me. But Bartolomeo was clear about what he saw, so maybe...*

Duccio and his wife as well as the Buccinis stayed at their tables.

Elisabetta spoke first, "I am glad that I had the opportunity to tell the truth."

Her father said, "*Sì*, when you looked the judge in the eye and spoke so loudly, I felt that you are innocent."

Duccio ventured, "When you kicked me under the table, Taviana, I thought I might become even more crippled."

Taviana laughed a little, and Duccio said, "I want to lighten your mood. I think that the judge will find us not guilty, but I wonder why he didn't ask me the same question he asked Elisabetta."

The massive door to the courtroom creaked and in walked Mimmo. He came to where the group was huddling and asked, "Is it over? Did you win?"

Taviana took Mimmo's hand, "No, dear Mimmo, we are just waiting for the judge's decision."

Bartolomeo had walked out of the courtroom and searched for Corporal Olivetti. He was nowhere to be found in the immediate vicinity. *I feel like Judas who took the pieces of silver and betrayed Jesus. Dear Madre de Dio, I pray that these two people will be found not guilty.*

⚜

When the early afternoon bells rang, the bailiff again said, "All rise."

The judge returned with his flowing robes, and all were asked to sit again so that he could read his verdict. From several pages of parchment, the judge read his prepared statement, "I have seriously considered the accusation of adultery against Duccio di Buoninsegna and Elisabetta Buccini. I know that this case was not brought into court, because of Elisabetta's acting as an apprentice. However, I do think that this has something to do with the case. I have checked the rules and have found that there are no specific guild rules against allowing females to be apprentices. As we know, some females work in the trades to support their children---if they do not have a husband."

The judge took a deep breath and looked at Bartolomeo. "The reason I bring up this issue is that I have concluded that Bartolomeo's "eye witness account" may have been distorted, because a woman was allowed to do a man's work and he was suffering without a job."

Then the judge looked to the back of the courtroom where Olivetti had quietly returned to his bench. After making sure he locked eyes with those of Olivetti, he looked down and continued reading, "Furthermore, when I heard the name of Corporal Olivetti being involved in the situation, I became quite suspicious of the motives and validity behind these charges. I have been the judge for two of the many cases in which the Corporal has gone to great lengths to punish Duccio di Buoninsegna for not attending musters of the military."

Looking at Duccio, the judge continued, "The man has paid his fines and is too old to serve now…no offense, *Signore*…"

All but Corporal Olivetti let out a small snicker.

"I don't exactly approve of the choices Duccio has made about the military, but he has made a definite contribution to Siena by giving us our magnificent Maestà that everyday brings praise to our Lord and the Blessed Mother.

Speaking of the Maestà, I actually walked the eight blocks or so to the Siena Cathedral during our recess, and I looked at the angels in the Maestà. Yes, they are all Elisabettas, and this backs up Duccio's claims as to what he was doing with her after workshop hours. Elisabetta had to disguise her identity during the day, but after the other apprentices went home, she could pose for the pictures of the angels."

Then the judge fixed his eyes on Bartolomeo, "As far as the witness' testimony that he saw Elisabetta staying after the candles went out, I simply don't believe him. I think that *Signor* Rubino is just a man that has fallen on hard times and regrets having taken the money---that I will call bribe money----given to him by Olivetti."

The judge breathed deeply and said loudly, "The adultery charges against Duccio di Buoninsegna and Elisabetta Buccini are therefore dropped. However, I hereby fine Corporal Olivetti twenty *soldi* for engaging in a vendetta against these two innocent people. Furthermore, Corporal Olivetti, you are banned from ever bringing a charge into a Sienese court again." Everyone in the courtroom gasped at once.

Then he looked across the room and gazed into Olivetti's eyes, "Do you understand?"

Olivetti shook his head, "Yes."

The judge went on to explain: "Most of you have probably heard that our Sienese courts are overrun by people making exaggerated and sometimes totally false charges based on a grudge. And I am sure you have heard of how we now penalize people who are guilty of participating in a vendetta. That is why you---Corporal Olivetti---are the guilty one in this room."

Banging his gavel on his desk, the judge said, "This court is hereby adjourned."

Duccio and Elisabetta hugged their respective families and stayed seated for a while to soak in the good news. The witness took a deep breath and smiled. Olivetti hurried out of the courtroom and went to one of the offices to make arrangements to pay his fine.

As Corporal Olivetti made his way out into the street he tried to examine his feelings. *I feel so imbarazzato...all of those people probably laughing at me.* He sat down on a stone bench where no one could see him. *I lost. All of these years I have tried to punish Duccio, but I have lost, and I can never plan a case against him again. It's over.*

Olivetti lost track of time, but eventually he arose from the bench and, as he hobbled home, he took deep breaths. At first, they were short and deep, but then they slowed down. His shoulders fell slightly, and his jaw dropped as it unclenched. *What's come over me? I don't know what is happening but maybe it's... relief... I can't try to punish Duccio anymore ...although I don't know what I will do with the rest of my life.*

Then from a bakery on the way home, Allesandro smelled the fresh bread he had allowed himself to taste just recently. He stopped in to purchase a loaf and took large bites from it. He heard the late afternoon bells of his local church ringing and for the first time noticed their melodious highs and lows. He momentarily felt the physical touch of a little boy who had bumped into him while chasing a ball. He thought of his great nieces and nephews who looked to him for occasional attention---which he had previously withheld. And then Allesandro thought, *Perhaps there is life after Duccio...*

PART SIX

SEPTEMBER 27, 1311-
APRIL 19, 2013

CHAPTER 33

SEPTEMBER 27, 1311

Father Giacobi waited for the opportunity to deliver a sermon especially for the ears of Taviana and/or Duccio. Taviana was a regular attender; Duccio was not. Finally Taviana appeared and, even though Duccio wasn't with her, Giacobi knew that she would carry news of his message to her husband.

After he genuflected and crossed himself, Father Giacobi began: "I know how much you all love the beautiful Maestà altarpiece that you see right behind me. I remember the great parade and the excitement in our city when it was rolled via oxcart into our beloved Siena Cathedral on the day of its installation."

"But I have to be honest with you. There were some things I liked about the Maestà and some things that I didn't…"

The crowd murmured.

The priest pointed to the altarpiece. "I had little doubt about the way the Holy Mother is depicted. She looks very regal while just a little bit human."

Then he pointed at the figure of Jesus. "The way young Jesus is depicted isn't exactly beautiful, but I appreciate the way Duccio di Buoninsegna portrayed Him in a way that showed He would be a wise man some day."

"Also, I like how the artist painted our local saints on the front. Until now, these martyrs were not shown quite so...so believably...like the real human beings they were."

And then Father Giacobi pointed to each of the martyrs as he said: "You see our patron saint Savinus whose hands were cut off...Ansanus and Crescentius who were beheaded...and Victor who was tortured to death---all during the persecutions of our early believers... some nine hundred years ago. Each of these men is painted in the way he could have looked while on earth."

"There is so much more that the front of the Maestà can tell us... about the apostles, the prophets, the angels and the life of Mary and Jesus."

Then the priest hesitated and lowered his head slightly.

"What has caused me trouble is the back of the Maestà."

He continued, "In a moment, I am going to have you follow me to the rear of the altarpiece, but first I need to make some comments."

"I originally thought the back of the Maestà was very bad...almost evil..."

The congregation gasped.

"Not because of anything really sinister but because it caused people to point at it and laugh sometimes...but I am beginning to feel that maybe... maybe...I was wrong..."

The people looked at their shepherd with wide eyes.

"So, let's look at the back of the Maestà together now."

Following the priest's movements, the large crowd made a slow, orderly shift around the piece to view it from its rear. "Just gaze on this side of the Maestà for awhile."

As best as each could see, the worshippers looked closely at the people, the actions and the landscape in the forty three individual paintings. And, yes, there was the occasional quiet laughter as someone saw a friend or acquaintance depicted as a prophet or judge or whatever. They also pointed at and whispered about the buildings from Siena and the black and white *balzana* Sienese insignia on the city gates.

"Your smiling and your laughter about seeing Jesus elbow to elbow with people like your friends and in a city that looks like ours…well…it used to bother me," the priest said, and the people became very quiet.

"But now it doesn't. Recently my family and I experienced an example of God's love through the actions of a human being."

The people smiled, and the priest said, "Yes, I have a family too."

He continued, "I'm not going to tell you who this person was, but I look at it as though he allowed Jesus to work through him, just as if… Jesus was right at his elbow.

This experience made me feel that the closer we can feel to God in our everyday lives the better we may be as people…If we ask ourselves what our Dear Lord would have us to do in the smallest of ways, perhaps we will be kinder and more virtuous…And maybe we won't have to worry about knowing a lot of rules…or doing things just right…maybe if we let God take our hand like He is right next to us…we will just know what to do…

Therefore, I apologize to the artist of the Maestà for not initially appreciating his work…and I encourage you now to look at the human side as well as the holy side of our beloved Maestà…and I won't reprimand you if you occasionally smile while gazing upon it."

❈

Taviana just about ran home after the service. She went through the workshop door and approached Duccio from behind while he was drawing at his desk.

She could only say, "*Mio sposo*," as she tried to get back her breath.

"Taviana, is there something wrong?" Duccio said as he stood up and put his arm around her.

"No, no, actually everything is *magnifico!* Father Giacobi said that he adores the back of your Maestà now! He wants all of us…" Taviana's breathing was still rough.

"Slow down, take a nice deep breath," said Duccio.

"I'm okay now, my dear. He said that recently someone was very kind to him and his family… and …and that made him think that if we just thought of Jesus being with us in everything we do…like in the Maestà… everyday… we would be better people."

"Ah," said Duccio as he beckoned Taviana to sit down with him and then took her hand. "Tell me more…"

And she did. Finally, Taviana decided to go upstairs and prepare lunch. Then Duccio ruminated about what he had just heard.

He had never shared with Taviana that the priest at Luca's funeral was his son, Father Giacobi. So much was going on right after he returned from the vineyard that he had forgotten to mention it. It dawned on Duccio that Giacobi did change, just as he had said he wanted. And now Duccio knew that it was Father Giacobi who had made and then taken back the perfidy charge.

As I've said to myself before," "It's the not knowing that will kill a man." Now that I know who was behind the perfidy charge and who was behind the adultery charge… maybe I can finally experience true Peace of Mind.

CHAPTER 34

1311-1318

In the next seven years before he died, Duccio lived to witness several major events.

Mimmo and Elisabetta ended up getting married---after their parents negotiated a dowry acceptable to everyone. The young couple lived with Mimmo's family. His parents moved up to the third floor of the family tower, and Elisabetta and Mimmo lived on the second story so that they could readily go down to the first floor that they made into their workshop. Elisabetta created painting after painting, and Mimmo used his salesmanship skills from working for Duccio to exhibit and sell her works on the street in front of the shop.

Elisabetta felt free to paint whatever she wanted and, as a result, she painted what she liked best---simple things from the immediate environment---which she endowed with great beauty. In passing by, travelers on religious pilgrimages were not interested in her artwork, but merchants from Eastern countries, such as China, adored and purchased her pieces. While Elisabetta never flaunted that she was a woman working in a man's world, she no longer took strides to hide her identity. And no one bothered her.

Duccio completed his Massa Marittima Maestà, and his patrons were pleased with the outcome. They especially extolled the sad beauty of the Crucifixion Scene that Duccio had created during the trial period--- when his muse Obsession had returned to him.

A few wealthy people also commissioned Duccio to paint small triptyches of Jesus and the Blessed Virgin with individuals from their own families depicted as disciples or other religious figures. To the delight of his patrons, Duccio executed these paintings with rich colors for the subjects' robes, realistic but flattering depictions of their family members, and gorgeous gilding with gold leaf.

However, in his last years of life, Duccio did not want to take any extraordinary risks in his artwork. Ever since the trial, he did not want to do anything to create a controversy that might endanger himself or his family. He was content that the Maestà was the centerpiece of the Siena Cathedral, that now all of the priests were supportive of it, and that it still instilled adoration in the eyes of the worshippers.

Duccio finally quit obsessing about his artwork and other problems in life. He began to experience the Peace of Mind he so ardently pursued all of his life. Trouble still followed him like an unwanted shadow, but Duccio felt accepting of nearly everything that came to him. The artist was surprised about something--- his creativity diminished as his serenity increased.

One of the things that brought Duccio satisfaction was that he noticed how potential patrons were receptive to the new styles and innovations introduced by his former apprentices. As could be predicted, Simone Martini created paintings of religious scenes that were exquisite, small and decorative. Pietro Lorenzetti combined Duccio's style of depicting people in their surroundings along with Giotto's love of revealing emotion.

Above and beyond the other apprentices. Ambrogio Lorenzetti painted in a style that was the most unique. His cityscapes expanded on Duccio's portrayals of Siena in the Maestà. But Ambrogio's city scenes were much larger than Duccio's, and the fact that he did not include any religious figures in his paintings was truly revolutionary.

Out of all the apprentices, Ambrogio was the one who made the most frequent visits to Duccio in the artist's last years. The two men always shared a few laughs, a couple of goblets of wine, and reminiscences about Ambrogio and Simone's wild stunts when they apprenticed for Duccio.

One day after Ambrogio had dropped by, Duccio told Taviana about his apprentices' successes. "I feel *contento* that by my trying new things and finally having them accepted--- this has made it easier for those boys."

"You have changed, *mio sposo*. I don't know why, but you are finally *contento* about just about everything. What do you think has happened to you?"

"If the truth be told, I am not trying so hard or wanting so much…especially in my art."

"Do you think that is a good thing…or a bad thing, *mio marito?*"

"I think it is probably…good…at this stage of my life, but now I am so glad that the Tension and Obsession that haunted me when I was younger were there…otherwise I wouldn't have had the…the need to create and the desire…to do it well…There probably would not have been a Maestà."

"That would have been disastrous!" Taviana exclaimed. "But now I am glad that you're finally getting that Peace of Mind that you always talked about. What did the priest say at mass about how everything has a…a season?"

"*Sì*, and I suppose I am in the winter of life…not much longer to go on this journey and …trying…trying somehow to enjoy every last step along the way."

"Ach! Don't talk like that. You will probably outlive our children," protested Taviana, but she turned away because she wanted to hide a tear or two creeping down her cheek.

Before he died, Duccio got in trouble one more time. In 1314, he was brought back to court for not repaying a debt. In his habitual desire to make his paintings perfect, he borrowed money to purchase gold leaf for a painting---a quantity that was above and beyond what had been predetermined by him and his patron. The patron promised to reimburse him but never did. In response to the court's order, Duccio slowly but surely paid the money back to his debtor.

Sadly, Duccio experienced poverty in the material sense in his last years. He just could never properly estimate what a work of art would cost him to do, and he always came up short when the job was done. However, he made it a priority to keep the vineyard going, and it reaped enough financial reward to break even, to pay Rosa and her family, and to keep Duccio well supplied with wine.

During the period of the adultery trial and all of his tension about how it would affect Taviana and Elisabetta, Duccio began having leg and back pain that progressively hurt more with each passing year. But even though his body ached and he had barely enough income---after his expenses---to feed himself and Taviana, Duccio still felt *contento*. Most of his children and grand-children came around frequently to visit, to gaze admiringly upon Duccio's latest project, and to help Duccio and Taviana with chores that were now difficult for them to do.

Everyday in the winter of his life, Duccio went down the stairs to paint in his workshop and then painstakingly up the stairs to spend the evening and night with Taviana. No matter how frail his health, he was not about to give up his art or his beloved wife.

In the middle of a stormy spring night, Taviana woke to the sounds of Duccio choking and gasping for air. Taviana yelled, "Duccio! Duccio!" She tried to hold her husband's jerking body steady so that she could breath air into his mouth, but it was to no avail.

"*Mio sposo, mio sposo*, don't leave me," she begged, but suddenly he froze and just stared unblinkingly outwards.

Taviana closed Duccio's eyes, forced his limbs back into a sleeping position, and held onto him for a while.

Finally she said, "Fly up, my dear Duccio, to see Jesus and our blessed Mother along with all of your beautiful angels, and I will come to see you soon." When she felt that Duccio's soul had departed, she slowly made her way down the stairs--- to send for Father Giacobi.

EPILOGUE

HEAVEN

A lot of people believe there is a heaven and that heaven is a place where its inhabitants are perpetually happy, reunited with their loved ones who made it through "the pearly gates," and only know of the good things concerning them back on earth. Imagine for a moment what this could be like for Duccio.

When Duccio first entered his eternal rest, he met his father and mother. His father said, "Son, you didn't have to worry so much about disappointing me. You made me proud---especially with the Maestà---and you brought honor to the family name," but then with a loving chuckle he added, "Why, though, son, did you have to get yourself in debt again at the end of your life?"

Eventually as each one of his family members entered heaven's gates at their own times, Duccio was reunited with Taviana, his seven children, and his many grandchildren. They all remained true to their faith in God that Taviana especially had inculcated in them. Two of Duccio's sons painted some well-received small panel paintings for churches in Siena.

His son, Tommè, who was the chimney sweep and preceded Duccio into heaven, said, "I should have listened to you, *Papà*, about the need to be careful after that black cat crossed my path, but I am thankful that you saved my brother's wife Rafaella and their unborn child when the sky turned black."

Duccio would have been informed that in later years he was given the title, "The Father of Sienese Painting." This was largely because of his great artistic achievements as well as the fact that he brought along or "fathered" three famous apprentices who made tremendous advances in the world of art.

He would have been made aware of how in 1336 Ambrogio Lorenzetti had fulfilled his dream and finally was commissioned by the Council of Nine to do two enormous frescoes depicting people in motion in their everyday lives---even though not one character therein was a religious one. He would know that these frescoes---entitled "The Effects of Good Government" and "The Effects of Bad Government"--- still adorn two giant walls of the Palazzo Pubblico today and have been viewed by massive amounts of people ever since their inception.

Ambrogio's Fresco About Everyday Life

Duccio would have learned that Pietro Lorenzetti developed a very successful career in the art world and that he and Ambrogio produced some highly regarded works together. The angels may have told Duccio one sad thing: that the brothers Pietro and Ambrogio both died at the same time from the Great Plague which hit Siena in 1338. They would have shared this with

Duccio, because he would be glad to know that at least the brothers died together.

He would have been told about the success of Simone Martini and how Simone eventually began painting some gigantic frescoes. Like Ambrogio, he was invited by the Council of Nine to do a huge fresco for the Palazzo Pubblico. His Maestà featured a scene of Mary and the angels that made them look like royalty bedecked with

Simone's Fanciful Maestà

flowing robes and gold ornamentation---surrounded by elegant foliage and decorative borders. Simone almost exactly copied Duccio's depiction of some of the saints and angels to put into his Maestà, but Duccio was more flattered than irate with the plagiarism. He was tickled to find that Simone ended up painting for a French king, spent his last artistic years with his wife in Paris and became a close friend of the famed poet, Petrarch. "Oh, how Simone loved those courtly ways," Duccio said to one of the angels.

Duccio was thrilled to learn how he and his Sienese School of apprentices formed a stepping stone from his Maestà in 1311 to the art of the Renaissance in the 1400's. Angels told him about Renaissance art and how it acquired the title of being "humanistic," because it portrayed human beings as having the capacity to think, learn and discover in new and exciting ways that hadn't been encouraged in the Medieval period when Byzantine art flourished. These new terms--- "Renaissance" and "Medieval"---fascinated Duccio.

However, it was not just his desire to make religious figures look "human" that was a contribution to Renaissance art. Duccio learned that his rendering of landscape---especially in the painting of Christ Entering Jerusalem---was a precursor to the use of "perspective" by Renaissance painters. Duccio had never even heard of the word, but he recalled how he had tried to make things look larger when they arc close and smaller when they are further away. He was allowed to peek into Rome and see how Raphael perfected Duccio's early use of perspective in The School of Athens painted on the walls of the pope's library.

"And, by the way," an angel told Duccio. "After you and partly because of you, artists began signing their names to their paintings or etching them into their stone sculptures."

But what pleased Duccio most about the Renaissance period was that artists still didn't forget about God even though they were concentrating so much on human beings. *I always had my doubts*, Duccio said to himself, *but regardless of my superstitions something kept telling me*, "There is a God." *Maybe that is why I made it to this paradise.* Duccio shed tears of admiration when the angels gave him a quick look at the Sistine Chapel scene in which God reaches out to Adam and breathes into him the gift of life.

Duccio never learned what happened to Mimmo, Elisabetta, Father Giacobi and Corporal Olivetti, because they were not real people. They were fictitious individuals created by this author to characterize the cultural and religious issues of Duccio's day. Although they were not real, I became quite attached to them and occasionally think about them still.

Over the centuries, Duccio became so busy enjoying his new life in heaven that he wouldn't have known about what was happening in his home city of Siena. For about a hundred years after his death, the people of Siena and neighboring city-states had a vibrant memory of Duccio---the great Sienese painter of the Maestà---but then that memory faded.

He would have been shielded from knowing that in the sixteenth century the Maestà was removed from the high altar at the Siena Cathedral. Somehow too its predella and pinnacles were lost.

He wouldn't have known that the widely read, sixteenth century art historian Giorgio Vasari gave Duccio no credit for his accomplishments. The Florentine did make a trip to Siena to view and to write about the city's most outstanding artwork. He had heard about Duccio but mistakenly was told that he produced a panel entitled, The Coronation of Our Lady, with paintings on its back and front. When Vasari went to Siena, he couldn't find it. By then, the Maestà had been put in a remote corner of the cathedral. In his art history book, Vasari only gave credit to Duccio for work he did not do---the colorful array of figurative tiles adorning the floor of the Siena Cathedral. In another error, Vasari reported that Duccio died in 1350, and he made the Lorenzetti brothers and Simone Martini the seniors of Duccio.

In 1711, the Maestà was taken from wherever it was stored at the Cathedral, and it was sawn into pieces--- some

Baby Christened At Contrada Fountain

of which were sold to various art collectors across the world. The pieces that remained were damaged in the process.

Today angels may or may not be shielding Duccio from knowing that the *contrade* are alive and well in Siena. People are christened in their *contrada's* fountain, still wear their *falsetto* scarves on important occasions, and cheer for their *contrada's* horses in Siena's twice -yearly Palio races. Actually, Duccio probably wouldn't mind knowing that the *contrade* remain an integral part of Sienese society today, because in the twenty first century they only serve a social and not a military function.

Girls with their Contrada Scarves

Duccio would be overjoyed to know that the city-states in the vast vicinity around Siena became unified in 1861 into what became known as the country of Italy. He would probably say, "It is about time."

It would be comforting to Duccio to know that in the last century or so some art historians have become very interested in Duccio again, and many outstanding art history books about the Maestà and Duccio's other known works have been published. Extensive research of the Sienese archives by a graduate student in Siena brought forth the specifics in this book about the court cases, the vineyard, the installation, and some of Duccio's commissions.

And, if he still cares about life on this earth, Duccio would be pleased to know that in 1951 an extensive restoration project bought back many of the auctioned-off pieces of the Maestà and cleaned up the six hundred and fifty year old masterpiece to make it look almost identical to how it originally appeared. The Maestà is now proudly exhibited at the *Museo dell'Opera* adjacent to the Siena Cathedral.

Last but not least, I ask for a word with you, Duccio, if you still look down here at times: "I tried to capture your heart and soul ---drawing from the chronicles and archives of your beloved Siena as well as your art. My main goal in this historical fiction novel was to bring to the attention of people in the twenty first century how you, Duccio, put together the largest, most dynamic religious altarpiece painting ever and how your artistic innovations helped pave the way for the art of The Renaissance. I just wanted to give credit where credit is way overdue and to join the throngs of people in Siena on June 9, 1311 who said, "*Molte grazie* for the Maestà."

SIENESE RECORDS Re: Duccio di Buoninsegna

To the best of my ability, I have ascertained the following information from reading archives and other records within a book by Jane Immler Satkowski entitled Duccio di Buoninsegna: <u>The Documents and Early Records</u>, published in 2000.

Due to frequent references to currency, I offer the following explanations. Twelve *denari* equaled a *soldo* and twenty *soldi* equaled a *lira*. However, the *lira* was a money of account and not an actual coin. The Sienese Merchants Guild set the daily exchange rate between the value of the *lira* and the *florin*.

d.=denaro, denari

s.=soldo, soldi

l. or £=lira, lire

f. or F.=florin

Satkowski used the following types of records:
Archives of Siena
Archives of Florence
Library of the Commune of Siena
National Library of Florence
Archives of the Siena Cathedral
Archivio Arcivescovile, Siena

DEBTS, FINES AND CHARGES VS. DUCCIO (A variety of Sienese recorders wrote down these facts; for the most part I have used their own words; some put in the exact date and some did not.)

1.) 1279---fined 10 lire for accusation made by Rodolfo Mangetti over financial loss and initiation of a lawsuit over property

2.) March-April 1280---100 lire for a condemnation (not specified) against him

3.) 1285---20 soldi because he was found by soldiers after the third sounding of the bells

4.) 1289---5 soldi for not being present at the meeting of the Council of the People

5.) 1289---10 soldi for not swearing allegiance to the orders of the Lord Captain of the Commune of Siena

6.) May 15, 1294---6 soldi and 8 denari for a fine (unspecified) levied against him in the amount of 5 soldi (due to not paying the fine against him for not being present at the Council meeting in 1289)

7.) June 5, 1294---12 soldi and 4 denari for still not paying the fine in 1289

8.) December 16, 1295---10 soldi on account of a fine for not paying back a debt to Lapo Chiari

9.) May 14, 1302---5 soldi on account of a debt

10.) December 4, 1302---5 lire for obstructing a street of the Commune

11.) December 4, 1302---18 lire and 10 soldi for not being present at any of the mustering of the Army at three different locations and for not standing at the watch of the guard at one of the locations

12.) December 20, 1308---Duccio agrees to pay back 50 florins from his large Maestà commission by the first of January to the Opera of Santa Maria of Siena; (this was in order to pay back a debt)

13.) 1309---100 lire penalty (reason not given)

14.) 1310---24 lire in penalties (reason not given)

15.) June 9, 1313---40 lire to be paid for over six months for a debt

MONEY PAID OUT TO DUCCIO:

1.) July-August, 1278---10 soldi for painting books of the Treasurer and the Four

2.) November, 1278---40 soldi for painting twelve coffers for documents of the Commune

3.) July-August, 1279---10 soldi for painting of the books of the Treasurer

4.) April 15, 1285---150 lire of the small florins paid out by the Society of the Laudesi for painting the Madonna at Santa Maria Novella Church in Florence

5.) October 8,1285---8 soldi for painting for the books of the Treasurer and the Four

6.) 1286---10 soldi for painting the books of the Four

7.) January 24, 1291---10 soldi for the emblems of the books of the Treasurer and the Four

8.) August 6, 1291---10 soldi for a painting for the books of the Treasurer and the Four

9.) March 2, 1294---10 soldi for painting the books of the Treasurer and the Four

10.) October 19, 1295---10 soldi for painting books of the Treasurer and the Four

11.) May, 1302---day labor payment for work he did with others for a Maestà in the Pisa Cathedral with Master Francesco as the chief artist

12.) December 4, 1302---48 lire for a Maestà and predella for the Chapel of the Nove on the ground floor of the Palazzo Pubblico in Siena

13.) October 9, 1308---Agreement for payment for the Siena Cathedral Maestà; Duccio was to receive 16 soldi per day with some money deducted in the early payments to settle a debt

14.) 1318---Taviana is referred to as wife of the late Duccio and being sole owner of half a house in which they had lived

The Front of Duccio's Altarpiece (without the predella and pinnacles

which became detached over the years)

From Art Resource

Close-Up of Mary with Angels

From Art Resource

The Back of the Altarpiece

From Art Resource

From the Back of the Altarpiece---Christ Washing the Disciples' Feet

From Art Resource

BIBLIOGRAPHY

Battisti, Eugenio, <u>Giotto:The Taste of Our Time</u>, World Publishing, Cleveland, Ohio, 1960

Bellosi, Luciano, <u>Duccio: The Maestà</u>, Thames and Hudson, London, 1999

Bunson, Matthew, <u>The Encyclopedia of the Middle Ages</u>, Facts on File Books, 1995

Carli, Enzo, <u>Sienese Painting</u>, Gallery Press, NY, 1956

Christiansen, Keith, <u>Duccio and the Origins of Western Painting</u>, Yale University Press, New Haven and London with the Metropolitan Museum of Art, NY, 2008

Corrain, Lucia, <u>Giotto and Medieval Art</u>, Peter Bedrick Books, NY. 1995

Eimerl, Sarel, <u>The World of Giotto 1267-1337</u>, Time Inc., NY, 1967

McEvedy, Colin, <u>The New Atlas of Medieval History</u>, Penguin Books, 1992

Norman, Diana (editor), "Siena, Florence and Padua, Art Society and Religion," 1280-1400, Vol. II, Case Studies, Yale University Press, New Haven, 1995

Satkowski, Jane Immler, <u>Duccio di Buoninsegna, The Documents and Early Sources</u>, Pacific Communications, 2000

Seymour, Frank, <u>Siena and Her Artists</u>, Longworth Press, Boston, 1977

Stokstad, Marilyn, <u>Art History</u>, 2nd Edition, Volume 1, Pearson Prentice Hall, New Jersey, 2005

Stubblebine, James H., <u>Duccio di Buoninsegna and His School</u>, Princeton University Press, Princeton, NJ, 1979

Van Marle, Raimond, <u>The Development of the Italian Schools of Painting</u>, Vol. II, Hacker Art Books, NY, 1970

Venezia, Mike, <u>Giotto</u>, Children's Press, NY, 2000

Weber, Andrea, <u>Duccio</u>, Konemann Verlagsgesellshaft, Koln, Germany, 1997

White, John, <u>Duccio: Tuscan Art and the Medieval Workshop</u>, Thames and Hudson, NY, 1979

ACKNOWLEDGEMENTS

My heartfelt thanks go to Tamie Holmes and Chris Babb who encouraged me to write this historical fiction novel. To Jan Faulkner, Evelyn Kupec, and Loredana Abramo who were kind enough to proofread it. To Anna and Vince Raimondi, my Italian-born friends, who made the necessary corrections to the book's Italian words and phrases. To Carol Tanzer who, along with Elliot and Peggy Spiegel, gave input on the book's content. To Linda Schehl and the librarians at the Lombard Public Library who helped me access the many art history books that I ordered from libraries across the country. To Kris Perkins who accompanied me in my research trip to Siena. To writing professor Kristine Miller for her honest but gentile critiques. To Loredana Manfredini-Verrilli and Mirta Pagnucci from College of DuPage who made the study of the Italian language and culture so enjoyable. To Joanne Blaze for her technical expertise. To Heidi Reichl who graciously allowed me to include her vineyard photographs. To my granddaughter Maya who eagerly asked me everytime I saw her, "Is the book ready yet?" To Rocco Blasi and Beth VanOpdorp who offered early advice. And to my daughter Jill McClain who so perfectly designed the front and back covers for this book.

31387838R00122

Made in the USA
Charleston, SC
15 July 2014